Fires of Brigantia

Tina Zee

DreamEngine Publishing

This edition published in 2022 by DreamEngine Publishing.
ISBN 978-1-915212-05-4

Email: publishing@dreamengine.co.uk
Website: DreamEngine.co.uk
Social Media: @DreamEngineuk

Twitter: Tina_Zee_111
Facebook: Tina Zee
Website: Tina Zee
Illustrator: info@louisetodd.com

To my family; Laura and Scott, Daniel, Sharnie, Matthew, and Joseph. And of course, Kevin, my beloved.
The best thing that ever happened to me.

"Is life so dear, or peace so sweet, as to be purchased at the price of chains and slavery? Forbid it, Almighty God! I know not what course others may take; but as for me, give me liberty or give me death!"

...Patrick Henry

PROLOGUE

Cartimandua was Queen of Brigantia, a powerful warrior tribe in Albion. From 43 AD to 69AD she became the crown head and overlord of adjoining tribes, thereby expanding Brigantia to cover the whole of northern Britain. It spread over the land between the River Tyne and the River Humber, and it extended from the Irish Sea on the west coast to the North Sea in the east. Brigantia became the largest Brythonic Kingdom in ancient Britain, [Albion].

Its people, the Brigante consisted of tribes and disparate groups who had settled all over the area. They came together to fight a common enemy, the invading Romans, but in equal measure, they would fight against each other. Cartimandua allied herself with the Romans as they moved to occupy Britain, and as a result the Romans allowed her to keep her lands and continue to rule her people. She became rich on the proceeds of this alliance, paid by the Romans to help them keep at bay the marauding tribes north of Brigante borders.

The queen had a reputation for immorality, taking whatever lover might appeal to her at the time. It was rumoured that she had illegitimate daughters, but little is known of them. When she replaced her husband King Venutius with his servant, the much younger Vellocatus, the royal house was shaken, and many aristocrats would not accept a former servant as their king.

More than this, she lost the trust of her people, most of whom hated the invading Latins, and despised their way of life, and so during the governorship of Aulus Didius Gallus (52-57AD), Cartimandua's ex-husband Venutius gathered an army of supporters, and rebelled against her and her rule, waging civil war against her and the invaders, and rallying the outraged Brigante tribes. The Romans sent troops to defend Cartimandua, and in return for their support, Cartimandua handed over Caratacus, ruler of the Catuvellauni tribe, and thereby depriving Celtic Britain of its most determined resistance leader. Aided by the Romans, Cartimandua put down the rebellion. In 69AD Venutius once again returned to take the Kingdom. This time the Romans were able to send only auxiliaries, who succeeded in evacuating Cartimandua but left Venutius and his anti-Roman supporters in control of the kingdom. Cartimandua is heard of no more. This story unfolds during these troubled times.

"Neither before nor since has Britain ever been in a more uneasy or dangerous state. Veterans were butchered, colonies burned to the ground, armies isolated. We had to fight for our lives before we could think of victory."

— The Roman Tacitus

"The Celts were fearless warriors because they wish to inculcate this as one of their leading tenets, that souls do not become extinct, but pass after death from one body to another..."

—- Julius Caesar

CHAPTER ONE

SGAILEAN DORCHA
Dark Shadow

O UT OF THE CORNER of her eye, she knew it was waiting. She could feel the breath, soft and warm; almost tangible against the morning sky, like the breath of a small doe standing motionless as it sniffed the air, alert to danger. It moved silently, slowly, taking one small shift forward, matching the rhythm of the beat of her heart. She knew that if she moved the spell would be broken, but move she must, for if she did not, then catastrophe would ensue.

She had waited long into the night on many occasions, daring to hope that one day she would catch a glimpse of the shadow. So close was it to her that often she had grasped the air, convinced that she would capture the phantom in her hands as she softly reached forward. But each time the shadow disappeared behind the wind.

Every day she remembered the impossible mission she must complete. The wind had blown hard and dangerously on that morning, whipping up a storm in the mist along the ridge. She knew she had to climb carefully, each step placed wisely among the loose stones and moss. She felt her way, cautiously avoiding hare holes and ditches. Her shoes were worn and unlaced. She wrapped her cloak over her head and around her shoulders, tying it securely so her face was protected from the battering rain. She remembered the precious bundle that she carried in a reed basket as she walked on into the darkness, hoping against every dark helpless feeling, that there would be a welcoming light in a not-too-distant place. The route had been planned with precision. She knew that lives depended on her safe arrival at the refuge;

that enemy hordes were ready to fight to stop her progress. She knew that she needed to escape the fires that raged behind her.

Protecting the opening of the cargo bag with her body, she could hear the whimpering of the frightened child. With determination and urgency, she faced the weather.

There was only one way for her to go.

She was unsure how long she had been stumbling along before she realised that this was no ordinary storm. The blue-green light of the mist gave off an eerie glow. She knew the Druids would be watching her through the fairie fog. All her nerve ends stood on edge and her thoughts were rapid, checking the path and checking the child.

They say that the darkest hour is just before dawn, and so it was that the dark became deeper, and the storm became stronger. Breathless now as the wind took her energy, she wept with determination and frustration as she battled against the forces.

But then, without a warning, she saw the shape, solid and mystifying, dancing before her. She stopped dead. Mesmerised by the sudden soft sounds of vibrations travelling through the air, like a breeze caressing her ear, she watched the image cast in front of her as it moved in rhythm with the ghostly strains. She felt the compulsion to dance. She knew in her right mind that this was a foolish thing to do, but her mind began to feel light, and her feet began to lift and float. She opened her arms to embrace the moment…

… and the shadow snatched the basket quickly and mercilessly.

She stumbled. Behind her was destruction. In front, only the black enveloping thickness of fear as she floundered. Dawn was breaking. The child was gone; was but a shadow.

FOUR YEARS EARLIER

Bianna emerged from her mother's room, leaving the ailing lady at rest on the feather pillows and soft blankets, atop her high bed. Her mother slept heavily as Bianna closed the oak door and silently made her way to the Great Hall and through to the kitchen and scullery at the back of the house. She knew that soon her brother would arrive, and she must prepare for the visit. She also knew that Edric would be tired and probably angry at being summonsed home on the feast day of Veteris, but she was acutely aware that the life in this world gifted to their mother was now short, and the festival was a time to reflect and forgive, and to visit with loved ones — both living and dead. She wanted to give Edric the opportunity to make his peace with the Lady Cynifrida Bloodeworthe before it was too late in this world. She doubted that the headstrong Edric would appreciate being summoned from the feasting, drinking and trollops dancing in the fields among the tents and marques, but it was a risk she was willing to take, to afford him the chance to pay his last respects.

As Bianna entered the scullery, two young girls, themselves not much younger than Bianna, jumped up and bobbed a knee. Bianna greeted them with a smile.

'We have a lot to do this morning, and you will have to help me with the grand hall decorations.' Yetta and Osma bowed again. They would do anything for Bianna, not least because although Bianna was only sixteen years old, she seemed wiser than her years; acting almost like a mother to them and the other workers and staff in the round house which was home.

The house of the Chieftain was the largest house of the thirty or so within the enclosure. It was built next to a second smaller houses situated so closely together that the pair of them had become one. The whole therefore accommodated two bedrooms, a hall with fire, and a small stall which had become the servant room. A smaller thatch house to the rear served as the kitchen, washroom, and scullery, and all was enclosed by a timber stockade, protecting both the house and the animals. Shelters round the inside of the stockade walls doubled up as stables and sleeping spaces for the stable hands, farm workers, and any others who might need shelter for the night. These areas at the back of the house and could be reached by walking round the inside of the wall fence. The whole warren of the lord roundhouses and shelters were accessible by only one main double door into the Great Hall, and from there each windowless room could be reached through oak doors. This was a luxury that Bianna's father had insisted on, making the bedrooms enclosed and more secure. He employed carpenters and joiners to make the doors and jams from solid oak, eight in all. Matching iron work depicted an eight-spoke wheel and a thunder bolt as a signal of the god of the tribe, Taranis: the god of thunder and master of war. Each piece of ironwork looked fierce and formidable. Wolf runes were etched over each door top, depicting battle scenes and sacrifices, as the god required. The Gabrantovices were a warrior tribe and were renowned for their ferocious ability on horseback, and their use of short glaives and swords. As a result of their expertise on the battlefield, they became known as the 'Horse Spirits.'

Cynifrida had lived all her life in this settlement, on the east coast overlooking the Northern Sea. Until his death, her father had been tribal leader of Gabrantovices, and on his passing, Cynifrida continued to dwell in the settlement with her lord husband Edwin *Beornraed*. There she birthed him a son, and daughter. She lived happily in Gabrantovices. Happy she was, at least, until the uprising when Beornraed's head was presented to the company, arriving home on the back of his warhorse with a note from the Queen of the Brigante: Cartimandua herself. Her consort husband, King Venutius, had become increasingly hostile towards the Romans even as Cartimandua made trade pacts with them. So, he roused enough supporters to attack Cartimandua at Isurium.

Edwin had left the settlement with a troop of his best men to pitch support for the queen's deposed husband, whose plotted revolt saw many men lost, and many homes razed. Anger against Cartimandua was high for what was seen as ceding to the enemy, but Cartimandua survived the rebellion, taking several of Venutius' relatives as hostages.

When Bianna's mother received the news of her husband's death, she moved into mourning and did not recover. Her heart was broken, and she wished so many times that she could be the one riding the horse gallantly out to meet the battle, and she the one to ride back decapitated instead of her dear-heart, Edwin. The note with the regal signature was attached by an iron staple to the right ear of Cynifrida's beloved husband. It bore pictures and drawings; a warning to anyone daring attempts at removing Cartimandua from her throne. The pig parchment spoke of more horrible deaths for sons and daughters who would dare to stand against her and her new love, the Roman arms bearer Vellocatus.

Bianna had been a mere ten years old when her father was killed by her own Brigantine queen. A few days later her brother Edric and the people in her settlement had lit the pyre as they stood round the red flames of the rick, singing in hushed tones, songs of love, of battle and revenge. People gossiped about the wrongness of the killing and wondered how it was that it had come about. Some blamed Edwin's father: an old tyrant of a man, who showed no love to either of his sons. Others blamed Edwin's brother, who could have come to Edwin's defence but did not. But overwhelmingly, the people in the sept that night could not and would not forgive their queen who had betrayed all of them to the invading armies of Latins from Rome. The blame lay unanimously at her feet.

Bianna had withdrawn from her world that night. It had been a world of love and safety; one of running and playing with her older brother; of fun practicing sling shots and playing 'stones' with the other children. There had been much laughter in that world. But that night, she entered a dark room in the recess of her young mind. She had not slept for many nights. The image of her father's blood flowing down the mane of his horse, mingling as a thick sticky mass of red and black hair would give way to waves of sickness and dizziness, to double vision and wakeful dreams. Many muddled images converged and left her numb. Her young thoughts could not settle. She would not allow them to settle, but on one thing, and one thing only: she would avenge the death of her father.

She lay on her bed and allowed her thoughts to take their own turn. Slowly the mist crept in; hazy at first, but sliding and forming, taking shape until she could see beyond the blue green ether. The figure stood in front of her. Bianna turned to rise but found the figure overshadowing her with a weight she could not shift. She was paralysed. Fresh images appeared in the fog, and she felt her mind rise from her body, as if she was a bird. She looked down to see a man wearing a black cloak, hovering near her bed. He was carrying a golden trinket box. The cloaked stranger tripped, and the box flew into the sky. A black eagle soared from nowhere to catch some of the trinkets as they spilled out of the sky. A crown appeared falling, falling from the golden hoard. Bianna searched in her mind for the crown, but the mist covered the ground, and she could not see through the thickness. She felt herself falling.

She awoke that morning knowing that something had happened to her but not knowing what. She sensed that something had lifted, and the image of her father had lessened as a new precedent embedded itself into her *anam*. She rose, washed, and began to take over her mother's pattern of life; the cooking and running of the household, the allotted garden and care of the goat and the pigs. All this, as her brother assumed his responsibilities for provisions and security. Each day she managed the small farm, organising the workers to tend the pigs and poultry, and the sheep on the pastures just beyond the sept and below the cairn. She planned the daily menus, the cooking and cleaning, while she cared for her mother, hoping she would one day see her return to health.

Bianna made bread, and cakes with the help of Osma and Yetta. They talked and laughed while they kneaded the dough. Bianna's long dark hair bounced in the flour several times, and as she flicked the plait away from her face, the flour billowed around the room in great clouds of white. It landed everywhere, to the delight of the giggling girls. 'There will be no flour left, if it all goes in the wind,' shouted Yetta as she picked up a handful of the white stuff and threw it up. A cumulus of powder filled the air and landed on the heads of the girls. They giggled more. Bianna smiled a broad smile. When Bianna smiled, the whole room lit up, and the world seemed right. The girls loved the company of their mistress and cared for her very much. As children growing up together, the difference in ranking had never been abused. Osma and Yetta appreciated the good and safe place they had been given by Cynifrida and the joy they had become accustomed to share with Bianna and Edric. They willingly embraced the happy home.

They stoked the fire in the middle of the room. Flames flickered upwards, drawn to the smoke hole at the top of the house. When the heat was right and the charcoal burned hot and dark, the half pig on the spit was wheeled round over the heat. The juices ran down and the flames sparked and splattered. Bianna organised the day. 'Osma, you are in charge of the spit. Turn it regularly, while Yetta and I fetch the platters and trays. We will be back to the kitchen to make cakes and sweetmeats shortly.' she said.

Bianna began to make ready the Great Hall. Yetta swept and cleaned the roof supports with rush besom. Osma swept the floors, bringing in fresh reeds to place as a covering over the clay base of the Hall. Yetta fetched candles and rush lights, filling the pots with oil, beeswax, and a little lavender to burn fresh fragrance into the dark room. The great table was set for sixteen people, though Bianna had no idea who would be joining them on this night. 'Probably Dubthach will come.' She smiled as she thought of the dark-skinned Druid and his long moustache. 'He always smelled of herbs and flowers.' she thought, remembering the aroma of him.

Most of the villagers had gone to the festival, but she prepared the room as if the feast was to be held there. At this point, Bianna thought about her mother, and swiftly took a drink and some bread out of the kitchen and straight to the ailing matriarch. She attended to her needs but was aware that Cynifrida was weak and unlikely to eat the food. Still, she put pillows under her mother's head and lifted her small way, so that she was able to take the juice Bianna had brought. There was little to no conversation. Bianna did what she needed to do but knew that there was little time between this world and the next for her mother. Once her mother was settled, she crept out of the room and back to the Great Hall.

As she returned to the Hall, smoke filled the room. Yetta must have lit the candles. She called out for her.

'Yetta, come. The candles are giving off too much smoke.'
But Yetta did not come. Bianna felt herself slump down against the oak door of her mother's room, coughing and struggling to breathe. Her lungs were on fire. 'No. Not me,' she told herself, as nausea overcame her. 'No. I must not die. I must be here for mother until she leaves this world. No. No. I cannot…'
A Druid came close, calling her name, 'Bian. Bian. Come with me. I will carry you.' She smelled the fragrant aroma of garden sorrel and juniper, before hearing the soft voice of Dugall Dubthach, her mentor and tutor of Druidic traditions. She felt safe in his arms. As he lifted her from the floor and carried her out into the fresh air, she gasped, and felt the air cut her like ice. At that moment, dizziness took her. She felt herself being lifted high, and then higher still, until she was on a level with the treetops. She could see the village, the smoke coming from the houses. She could hear Yetta calling for her, and running out of the house, looking for her. A shadowy figure of a man in a black cloak came out of the door and stopped Yetta. From her lofty position, Bianna saw a flash of gold and a box hidden under the cloak of the man. She had seen that box before. Yetta quickly took the box, hiding it under her skirts before disappearing into the house.
A distant voice spoke, 'Yetta has the box. She will keep it safe. Leave it with her, for now, but come back and fetch it when the time is right.' The Druid laid Bianna on a blanket by the door and walked away. Yetta and Osma fussed round Bianna for a good while before she came round.
'What shall we do?' asked Osma.
'Bring water and a cloth. I will bathe her forehead with cold water and herbs. Bring the burning rushes and mint leaves. We can waft them till she smells the infusion. That will surely wake her.' Sure enough, Bianna slowly came back into her senses. She sat bolt upright and stared at Yetta.
'You have something precious Yetta, and one day I will require it of you,' she said. Then softly, almost silently, she began to sing the old song, the *giedd*, which had been sung so many times to her by her mother when she was in her cradle. She knew it in her heart. It whispered forth as the wind blew. She rocked back and forth, repeating the first lines — forgetting the others, she rocked back and forth…

When boar and eagle meet,
At the brown and boar seat,
Though death and loss lay hand in hand

7

FIRES OF BRIGANTIA

Our soul torn in a thousand strands...
The god of fire will rise.'

Bianna knew that Yetta hadn't the faintest idea what she was talking about. 'My head is all foggy,' she said, as she rubbed her forehead. 'You know it sends me mad, sometimes,' she mumbled.

CHAPTER TWO

AITHRIS

Rite

EDRIC WAS A FEW YEARS older than Bianna. He was a strong boy who enjoyed life to the full. He was known for his lusty appetites for all things, and for his hot temper. Manu fights ensued after the death of Edric's father. The people in his tribe belonged to the camp that hated the Romans, and the threat of invasion. But there were as many other *septs* that the Romans had infiltrated, bribing with gifts and tokens to bolster support that they were building across the land. Edric loved to goad these other camps, riding out on a day's adventure, causing havoc and annoyance as often as he could. He had a small band of followers, boys of thirteen or fourteen years old, who joined him in the pig-pokery and petty theft of anything near to hand. Eggs were often thrown over walls and mud left in doorways. His band of lads grew together and played together. Edric, a born leader, ranked his 'men' according to his needs and their ability. He gave rewards for bravery and daring out of the wealth of his father's trophy hoard.

Buite, the most daring, was constantly by his side. Beored, his second. A handsome jovial boy was followed by Cerdic and Wulfnud who were happy to be the *folgiere,* taking orders easily from Edric. Tiernan was the runner. Edric always pointed out to Tiernan that the runner was probably the most important warrior, as he was the one who took on the most dangerous of warfare, spying out the land before attack, and getting reports back swiftly. Edric chose him as the runner mainly because he was very small in stature, enabling him to spy easily. He could crawl into the smallest of holes or hide behind a tree

9

trunk without any of his anatomy showing. Edric called him Tiernan the Tough, though often they would taunt him, calling him Tiernan the Tiny, or Tiernan the Timid, ridiculing him more that the lad deserved.

When they were younger, Edric had devised a 'warrior test,' where the lads had to undergo some feat of bravery to prove their aptitude in battle. One such test happened when Edric laid out a plan to kill a rabbit they had captured. The others had cornered the buck using their shields. Edric ordered his elfin sized friend to be tough and kill the 'enemy'. But Tiernan could not. Shaking his head and looking at the buck, he took steps away, until his back hit a tree. Edric, angry at the lack of obedience, took out his dagger, and threw it toward the tree. It hit the tree but sliced the top of Tiernan's ear clean off. Blood gushed form the wound. Tiernan turned and ran into the woods and away, Edric called after him 'Tiernan the Timid! You are a coward and are not worthy to be called a Brigante warrior.' But for all Edric's bravado, guilt swallowed him up.

As he disappeared into the thicket, Tiernan shouted, 'You wait and see. One day, you will pay!' The boys laughed as he ran, but that was the last they saw of Edric's scout.

Edric was building a reputation for being arrogant and ruthless, but he was an expert horseman, having ridden since he was small. He knew how to handle his steed to get the best out of her. His timing and agility on horseback made him almost impossible to catch. He was someone people watched. Sometimes with admiration, and sometimes with hatred and jealousy. Full of bravado, the young warrior lapped up any and all attention, fearlessly taking arms against anyone who dared to stand in his way. Edric's only challenge, only fear, was of the fleeting shadow which seemed to hover over him in times of darkness.

As Edric was approaching eighteen, he was to enter the full rite of passage of a Brigante warrior. The feast of Veteris during the festival of Litha, was a welcome distraction from the small, everyday skirmishes and conflicts between the Brigante and the Roman soldiers, and Brigante *sept* against Briante sept. This was a time when man and boy met for a different type of madness. The festival was a time when young and old gathered to sacrifice to the warrior god, make jousts and arm wrestle, arrange weddings and trade between septs. The whole of Brigantia celebrated this festival, (except when they were at war), though primarily it was a time for the warriors to show off their prowess in the ring, and for egos to be inflated. The *braint* and commoner alike gathered for the fighting matches and fun.

Two days earlier, Edric had packed his magnificent horse with all the items necessary for the journey to the main festival arena, and he had set off with two of his followers, Buite and Beored, the ones among his band of followers who Edric most favoured. He had set out with a will, to capture the heart of a young maiden, to bed as many other maidens as is possible in a short space of time, and to win some of the rewards for fist fighting and wrestling. He also intended to take the challenge of fire walking and rites laid down by the Kings of Brigantia over years of tradition. This would prove he was ready to take on the cloak of manhood and claim his bride. He set off that morning, full of hope and excitement, and full of determination to make the name of Bloodeworthe resonate among the elite in Brigantia.

He had only just unpacked his travel lit in one of the clay huts erected for the festival, when Buite came running across the field shouting. 'Edric. Edric. I have news from home.'

Edric lifted the canvas tent door and looked out. 'What's the rush?' What have you heard?'

Buite was out of breath, but managed to splutter out, 'I've just seen Wulfnud. He's traveling from home with the Druids and he has a message from Bianna. You have to go home, Edric. It's your mother!'

Edric stopped short to think about this, and without a hare's breath between thought and spoken word, he responded, casually. 'Later Buite. Later. I have a few things to do first. When all is in its place, then I will return.'

Buite added anxiously, 'But Ed, your mother may well go before the sacrifices, and it will be too late to see her through into the new dawn. You must go now.'

'The timing will be right, Buite. Don't fret. We have till the dusk, surely,' and Edric went back to the tent to continue unpacking. But anger seethes inside him. He would miss the fire walking and the rites if he went too soon, and it was his future at stake here. He remembered all the years since his father's murder when he had been waiting for this time to arrive. This time he would emerge as a man and a warrior. This time he would not let his mother hold him back, as in previous years, even if it meant he would not be there at her deathbed. He swore under his breath.

The urgency of the message from Bianna asking him to return had eluded Edric almost immediately when he saw the young girls. A crowd of beauties made their way toward the boar-ring. He jumped upon his black horse and positioned the stallion in front of the women. Touching the amulet of Taranis on his chest, he bowed, first checking the faces of the four.

'Good afternoon, fair maidens. Have you come far today to see the wonders of the 'Mighty Men?' Edric alluded to the famous fighting warriors from the Corinota tribe, reputed to have slain more than sixty Roman soldiers with bare hands. The girls giggled and looked sheepishly at the handsome young fighter, dressed in skins of boar and badger, arms bare and chest uncovered displaying his well-defined muscles. Edric's hair fell long and dark over his shoulders, tied back with a leather strap. His eyes, a piercing blue, looked from one to the other of the young faces before him. His mind was choosing which one he would have first. His body, virile and strong, was hot with the thought of it.

'We have come with our lord and master, Beornbran Byrde. He is one of the braint, who come to battle tonight against the wraith shadows as the moon rides high. Will you also be battling tonight, sir?' For a moment, Edric felt arrogance flick at his heart and he wanted to respond by aligning himself with Beornbran. But an apparition of Bianna begging him to return home leaped across his mind causing him to falter.

'I will not have that pleasure, fair ladies. I must return home tonight, for my mother is ill and may not recover. I need to be at her bed when the god's fetch her. But I hope to see you again.' With this, Edric turned, flicked a nod to his men, and sped off toward the north, a route bound for Gabrantovice. He travelled for three hours along the old route back toward the coast, but the night caught up with him, and darkness fell like a druid cloak. Edric sensed eyes following him, watching, from the depths of the darkness. He raced until the horse could go no further.

Slowing his steed as he approached a small hamlet, he saw that the inn door was open, and the light of many candles shone into the darkness. Edric dismounted, wrapped his cloak round him, covering his body with the badger fur before looking inside the inn. A few travellers were sitting round the fire, and beyond them the booth keeper filled flagons with barley ale and beer straight from the barrel by the back stall. Two lasses served the travellers and chatted amongst themselves.

Edric moved to sit at one of the benches placed round the room, his intentions to seek refreshments. But just as he seated himself, another traveller entered behind him.

This traveller was tall, heavy, and wild looking, sporting earrings and stone chains around his neck and head. His feet were clad in leather boots, but they were worn thin and had long ago seen the best use. His cape was wrapped over his shoulder and fastened with an iron pin, much as a Roman soldier might have worn over his uniform. The man's sword hilt and axe were in plain sight beneath his cape. He had a girl with him, shackled by a thick rope tied to his wrist. She hung her head so that her mass of red hair hid her face. He pulled her in to his side and together they walked to a bench. They sat in silence, while the wild man's eyes darted round the room, assessing potential danger. The girl complained of thirst and exhaustion, but the wild man just tugged and grunted at her. Tension in the room was palpable. Edric avoided his eyes, looking toward the booth keeper and nodding his assent for beer. One of the lasses came over to him with a tankard and almost flung it onto the bench. She asked him where he was from and where he was going. Edric, wary, answered only in part, keeping his intentions secret, should they be overheard. Edric had one ear tuned toward the wild man and his captive, as the other lass went to serve him. Pressure in the room grew as the wild man bellowed across to the keeper.

'Bringmebeer. And water for 'er. Bringmebroth, wi' bread,' he grunted.

'Should I bring broth for her?' asked the lass.

'No. She can 'ave what I leave.' And for good measure, he slapped the girl's thigh. The girl jumped in pain and whimpered in fear, but the wild one slammed her back down on the bench.

'Shut it, or I'll finish you off. One way or another…I don't care which,' he growled, as his hand went up her skirts. Edric felt his chest tighten. Clenching his fists, he breathed deeply to control his anger. Having seen so often the brutality used toward women by bullies and thugs, even in his own *sept,* his skin crawled. He had promised himself that he would always treat ingénues with care and kindness. Come the day when he was lord of his people, he would teach them also how to consider the other person compassionately. He called from across the room, 'Anyone want to drink with me?' He banged his tankard on the bench to attract attention. Looking toward the rough captor, he shouted, 'What about you, Sir? What's your name?'

The man stared at Edric, as if deciding whether he should be bothered by this interaction. The girl shouted, 'It's Taexalin the Wild.' He raised his hand as if to strike the girl for opening her mouth, but she dodged the attack, moving backwards to evade the strike. To prevent the girl's situation worsening, Edric redirected his conversation.

'Hey. She looks a good bit of skirt. Is she for sale?'

'Who's askin'?'

'Someone who would give good money for a night with her. I've missed the fun at the feast and could do with catching up. What's your price, sir?' he bartered.

'Show me the colour of your money, first.'

Edric stood as if to fetch his purse, and as he did so, walked over toward the man. As he reached inside his boar skin, he pulled out his dagger and deftly slashed the rope that held the young girl. In a flash she was up and out of the door. It took a moment or two for the wild one to realise what had happened before he was up and grabbing the cloak around Edric's shoulder. Edric spun round, freeing the badger skin and, kicking out his legs, knocked the great savage to the floor. He had no time to think about what he should do next, because the brute was back up on his feet and knocking the bench out of his way so he could grab Edric again. Like lightning, Edric jumped to avoid him. Wild against wild, the fighting continued, with grabs and punches on both sides. Edric slashed at the man with his dagger.

Just then, Buite and Beored entered the hut. They had been following a short distance behind Edric, as they always did. They burst into the fighting scene with swords drawn, ready for action.

'Ed. We are here.' And without ado, they surged forward toward the wild animal growling in front of them. Calling for help from the gods, Edric gave a final slash at the man's throat. Blood gushed down his chest and onto the floor, as Taexalin the Wild slumped down.

Edric snatched the amulet from around the dead body of Taexalin the Wild and sat back down at his bench. He looked at the heavy iron neck trophy that he would keep as proof that this night he had fought a battle and, victorious, had saved a maiden from a terrible future. This, a rite of passage into the warrior world he longed to join, was all he needed to prove his worth. He tied the iron talisman onto his belt. The two young men sat at his side. They slapped Edric on the back, congratulating him on his warrior ability. They drank long and fast of the beer, calling for more drinks all round. Even the other travellers joined in with praises for Edric and his two companions. The place became alive with singing and drumming of fists on the tables. The lasses got on the tables and danced. They danced round the body lying in its own red pool. A sense of relief spread across the room. Then Edric thought about the girl. He went outside to look for her and found her in a huddle by the door. She had been watching the fight.

'I prayed for you. By the gods, I prayed you would save me from that pig of a man.' Edric fetched some bread and water, and the girl began to relax a little.

'What is your name, girl? What is your story?' he asked.

'I am Maawan Boann, daughter of Cartimandua, Queen of Brigantia.'

'Yeah… And I am Taranis. God of Thunder,' Edric mocked. 'You had better come with me for safety, 'Princess Maawan.' Get on the back of my horse, and we can talk later. Tonight, we must get back to Gabrantovice.'

Buite and Beored followed as all four galloped into the night, arriving home at just before midnight. The candles were burning bright as Edric and Maawan rode past the village Druid Orders and entered the hall. Yetta woke immediately from her sleep and knocked Osma. They were standing before Edric even had his sword and dagger unhooked, and his skins off his back. Osma ran to stoke the fire, and soon the crackle of logs stirred again in the grate. Yetta brought food and wine to the table, and Edric thanked them both, signalling to Maawan to sit by his side, and eat.

'Where is Biann?' enquired Edric of the girls. 'Fetch her to me.'

The girls ran off to fetch Bianna.

Bianna had been in the back of the house listening for the sound of Edric's horse approaching. Running to the top of the sloping mound by the back of the washroom, she had watched for Edric's approach. A fog clouded her view but as it cleared a little, she saw the girl; a beautiful flame haired girl with golden cloak sitting on Edric's stallion. The stars shone round her head as a crown, and the ring on her finger showed a royal seal. A dark shadow hovered over her right shoulder, signalling danger.

The image disappeared, and Bianna was left alone, still waiting for Edric's return.

Osma found Bianna sleeping on the mound. Osma shook her and shook her. 'Biann, Edric is home… Wake up.'

Bianna jumped up to greet her brother, but the blood rushed to her head, and she swooned to the ground again. Osma ran to get water for Bianna, and then helped to steady her mistress as she entered the Great Hall. Edric greeted his sister with a kiss, and a bow.

'I came as soon as I could, little sister. As soon as I got your message, I made preparations to come home,' he said, knowing he was lying. But her call had been too strong for him to ignore, so he had obeyed.

'How is mother? Is…she…?'

'Yes, she is still with us, Ed. Go to her now, though, as time is running out. I will follow. The moon is rising, and the Druids are aware of her imminent passing. They will want to fetch her home soon enough.'

Edric moved toward the oak door, behind which his mother lay, but turned back to Bianna.

'Oh! I forgot to say. I have brought a friend with me; someone who needed my help on the way home.'

'Yes. I know, Edric. We will talk later. Go to mother.' Edric was puzzled by Bianna's reply, but deciding that he would enquire with her later, he entered the room where his mother lay between sleep and waking. She did not open her eyes but lifted her hand for her son to hold it. Edric approached the bed and took the old hand in his, kissing it with a gentle caring kiss.

'Mother,' he said.

With laboured breath, Cynifrida spoke softly to her son.

'My time has come, Son, and you must take the mantle of responsibility from my shoulders and wear it proudly for the sake of your father's name and for me. The name of Edwin *Beornraed* will remain strong in our tribe, and you will wear it with pride, and humility. Edric Ben Beornraed.' Edric kissed his mother's hand again and promised he would do what he could to make both her and his father proud. He promised to avenge his father's death, and to make the name of Bloodeworthe strong again.

'Fetch me the box from the stronghold, Edric.'

Handing the box to his mother, he lovingly caressed her hand. 'This ring was your father's and his fathers before him. Wear it with pride,' she said, handling the ring with care and affection. 'This amulet shows the family symbols; the gods of Taranis, of thunder and wheel.' She took out other trinkets and brooches made of gold and silver, bearing godlike symbols from long ago. Pointing to the symbols, she explained, 'All these gods will protect you and serve you whenever you have a higher order. This signet is mine, and I wish for Bianna to wear it. Please gift it to her when she marries.' She picked out a ring. The hoop of the ring was wrapped with fine wire to decorate, and each end of the wire formed a trumpet shaped finial. It was intricate and well-made. It had been Cynifrida's betrothal ring. She continued slowly, 'The coins and jewels are to be shared among you, for you to use as is necessary. But this parchment is for you. It bears promises your father gave to me on our wedding day. It tells of your birth, and the gift of standing as future Lord of Gabrantovice. Keep it close to your heart, for when you marry it proves your birth right. Should there be any doubt; search out Donn Donnlugh, the High Druid of Brigantia, who holds all secrets and mysteries. He will bear witness. He is under oath to swear the truth.

'Mother, why would the High Druid know about me?' asked Edric.

'Before your father was lord, Donn Donnlugh was here. He is from Gabrantovices, and a kinsman. He left to serve the queen when he fulfilled his Druid erudition,' she murmured. Then looking away she added, 'Watch his temper, and his enmity. They do not call him the

Dark Lord for nothing.' Edric moved to ask more, but, lifting one finger, his mother signalled for him to stop. 'Now I am tired, Edric,' she added, stifling a yawn. Tapping the parchment feebly, she continued, 'These promises given to me, given by your father are yours too, and I pray that your bride be one who will always love and serve you. Remember that your father and I always loved and protected you.' Cynifrida closed her eyes. Now whispering, she asked for Bianna.

With both her children round her bed Cynifrida took hold of Bianna's hand. A soft glow and beauty came over their mother that they had never seen before; a fusing of her young self and her dying body. Just as the moon reached its zenith, the room went dark, and the Druids appeared. Chanting as they moved, Cynifrida left this world.

CHAPTER THREE

BEANNACHD LEIBD
Goodbye

THE DRUIDS MARCHED silently into the room where Cynifrida lay, eyes closed, grasping the talisman of Tarantis and Brigga between her hands. They silently moved round the lady and began to prepare her body for the final farewell, and to prepare her soul for the future afterlife. Over her face they placed a linen cloth of white, and on her chest, they positioned a ceremonial cup, where mourners could gift coins and trinkets for Cynifrida to use in the next world. They placed holy leaves of alder, willow, and laurel at her sides, sprinkled with herb potions and holy water, sanctified at the shrines of the gods of the Brigantes. They whispered and chanted over the body, while, on hearing the news of their lady's departure, visitors came, one by one, to pay their respects. Even at that early hour, the people came.

Edric and Bianna stood silently at the side of the bed, taking it all in. Yetta and Osma waited outside the oak bedroom door, offering drinks and food to the people of the sept as they left Cynifrida. There was a silence over the whole parade; people coming and going in single file, heads bowed in respect; placing their offerings in the ceremonial cup, then taking the food gifts presented by the mourning family. For three hours the people came; many had returned immediately from the Festival of Veteris as soon as they heard of Edric's homeward call from the camps. For two more hours the people came, and then finally the Druids closed the door. The body would remain there until the morning light, and at noon the pyre would be built.

On the morning of burial, the High Druid of Gabrant-ovices, Dugall Dubthach came with his *fey* made of aspen. Runes and symbols were carved into it, showing the spirits' power in the rod, along with *Ogham* letters and symbols, the Druid language of magic and mystery. He waved the rod over Cynifrida's body, chanting and prophesying that the re-born lady and head of the tribe of Bloodeworthe would rise by the tree of fire and steadfastness. He took some little cones clinging to the branch of the alder set by her cold body. He lit a candle and placed the little cones in a circle round the flame, all the time chanting the old mysteries, in which he was unusually adept.

A Druid in brown cloak stepped into the room. 'I am sorry Dubthach, but I need to speak with you on a matter of some urgency. I think you will agree.' Dubthach looked round, his eyes wide with amazement that anyone should interrupt his rituals. The Druid continued, 'Should not the High Druid Donnlugh be notified of Cynifrida's passing? After all, he will be the one deciding who will be the next lord of Gabrantovices.'

Dubthach stood still for a moment before he answered. 'I think that at this stage, we do not need to approach Donnlugh. I think, we need to see how this day plays out.' Dismissing the Druid, he continued with his ritual, rolling his eyes at the impertinence.

Bianna had not slept more than two hours since her mother's death, and she had risen before the rooster. She began once again to prepare the Great Hall for the wake that would follow the funeral, and she needed to make sure that bread was baked, and meat was on the spit in readiness. She was surprised to walk into the kitchen and find Maawan already there; she had cleaned the fire grate of yesterday's ashes and was busy making scones. Maawan bowed when she saw Bianna, and moved toward a dark corner, away from the doorway that allowed but a glimmer of the morning sunshine to break through. Bianna ignored her. Bianna lit the fire then left the room to call for Osma and Yetta.

Maawan avoided Bianna when she could. She had to speak with Edric, but she realised, 'Today isn't the right time to get his attention.' She continued with the work that needed doing as a 'thank you' to Edric, and then she would make her arrangements to travel on.

At dusk, as the birds took their last flight to roost for the night, the candles were lit and Cynifrida's body atop the wicker coffin was lifted high by the company of Druids. A single drummer beat a steady proclamation, and in steady rhythm they marched toward the outer edges of the village. The Bloodeworthe household silently followed behind the

Druids, and then the people who knew and loved Cynifrida followed also. The warriors on horseback followed slowly. The farmers and villagers, iron workers, and arms makers all clapped in rhythm to the Druid march. The women and children followed too, wailing their grief as they all walked toward the *barp* outside the sept, and overlooking the mighty Northern Sea. Maawan walked with them, observing the movement but staying in the shadows.

Dubthach stood on a wooden dais where he could be seen by the grieving crowd that had gathered round the basket holding the body of their lady, now atop the pyre. He was an impressive, rather formidable man whose discernment was revered and respected. When he spoke, the people listened. A silence fell on the crowd as he began to sing *ecnaire* followed by an elegy; a poem praising both Edwin Beornraed, Lord Bloodeworthe of Gabrantovice, and her ladyship, Cynifrida. He recalled to the people his own love of the two leaders.

'I served Edwin and Cynifrida for almost all of my training years, growing with them as I learned the art of my profession, and they became your leaders, here in our much-loved sept. Now, as I reach my thirty-third year, I recall the many times I rode out with Edwin, to battle and to war. And in those times, I discovered the strength and courage which made the man. In troubled times, both Edwin and Cynifrida were always fair; always kind; their hearts, generous and forgiving. My Lady, Cynifrida brought peace wherever she walked. But the two united, wore the spirit of Brigantia as a vestment, tied to their hearts. Today as we bless their departed souls, may their spirit; the spirit of Brigantia, live on through each of us here today.'

The people came again with food offerings, rings, amulets, and coins, placing them on and around the wooden tinder, and then moving farther away from the circle. Dugall stood to one side, but beckoned Edric to come forward. It was time for Edric to take his place, so he climbed the platform to speak to his people. He raised a hand, seeking their attention, and the cairn fell silent again.

'This day,' he said, rather timidly. 'This day is the day when we acknowledge the passing of our lord and lady, my father and mother from this world to the next. They leave us bereft, but not without hope. For our future is driven by their desire for the good of us all. They taught us fairness and justice. They taught us to care and share. They taught us to fight for what is right…and fight we will.' Edric took a breath and looked round the crowd. The anger in his heart felt like a volcano in his chest. He clenched his fists as he continued. 'The Romans would take away our freedom, and our liberty. They would

21

take away our rights and our religions. Our Gods, they would take from us, and our way of life. Because of the Romans, our own Brigantine queen deserted us to side with their ways and because of this, my father was slaughtered as a bull in the ring.'

Edric hung his head and dropped his hand but continued with a power and passion unknown to him. 'This day,' he said, still with clenched fist, speaking low and hard to the crowd of mourners. 'This day!' he repeated louder, lifting his head, and showing a determined expression. 'This day is the day I avow revenge on Cartimandua, on the enemies of our tribes, and on the Romans.' At this, there was a low bubble of noise rising from the crowd before him. He knew he had their attention.

Maawan gasped as he uttered these words. She took a few long, slow breaths to calm herself, shrinking even further into the crowd, hiding in the midst of the company.

'This day, as a sign of the passing of my beloved parents, I will fight against the queen and all who follow her, until I return victorious or until I return to the ground to join both my mother and my father.' Lifting both hands as if to anoint the air. 'Who is with me?' he shouted. "Who is with me?' A great roar of agreement from the people ascended. One after the other, the crowd began to fall in front of Edric, bowing the knee and placing right hand against chest as a sign of allegiance.

Edric held his hand high again, and the crowd fell into silence, intent on listening to every word uttered from the mouth of their new lord.

'As your new chieftain, O' people of Gabrantovices, I promise to be fair in justice, honest in my undertakings, and always to put the needs of my people before my own. I will listen to the advice from our judges, the Druids, and take into consideration all that they say.' Turning to Dubthach, he nodded. Then, turning back to the crowd, he promised, 'I will give my life, if necessary. That the spirit of Brigantia may burn as an eternal flame within our hearts.' At this, the crowd cheered and jumped with delight.

Edric concluded, 'I will ask Bianna to light the fire, as we say farewell to my beloved mother. For a short time, we will watch, while the gods take Cynifrida back to themselves. Then we will return to our warmth and celebrate the passing; for the wheel of Taranis will continue; life, then death, then life again.'

Bianna lifted the torch high and moved toward the pyre, lighting it in three places: the head, the left, and the right. Dubthach walked with Bianna. She was comforted by his presence as she continued the ritual.

The other Druids followed, chanting the old sayings in Drueidan, praising the old gods of Brigantes. As the fire burned, the people knelt and began to sing the lilting tune, first sung by the 'Old Ones,' and remembered every dark day of death.

We lay our warrior on this mound.
Grief and fire to scorch the ground,
Beast and bird flee this night,
for woe becomes the dreadful sight.
When great souls die, our souls cry out,
'till rebirth brings the morn about.'

The flames rose high as the night set in, and the singing stopped. As the people began to wend their way back to the village, they heard a distant drum beating in rhythm with the sea, beating their return. Then music rose from the clearing in the centre of the houses. Bianna had arranged for musicians to play as the people returned from the funeral. She knew this was not wholly a sad occasion, but rather one where the people should also be celebrating life, and the new High Breehin, Lord Edric.

Bianna had instructed Osma and Yetta to bring the spits outside and roast pig and lamb had been cooking over the fire while the funeral had been taking place. Beer was wheeled round to the heart of the village and tankards were filled. Warriors and boys were praising the new Lord of Gabrantovice as they slammed tankard to tankard. Women were running round the place, bringing seats and benches out of their homes so the night could be enjoyed together. Food appeared from the lord's house, and from other houses in the village. Soon the whole sept was celebrating.

Maawan crept back to the house to gather her thoughts. 'My saviour's public declaration swearing vengeance for the death of his father, might include me, the illegitimate daughter of Cartimandua,' she thought.

Maawan had already lost her two older sisters, killed by her stepfather, Venutius as he raided the queen's oppidum in a coup against his estranged wife. Maawan had escaped his vengeance, hiding in a cart outside the fortress walls, then, when it was quiet and clear, she ran, and ran northwards. She had hidden many times since then but had always found somewhere to rest. Some of the tribes that were aligned to Cartimandua had taken her in and protected her. She had hoped that Edric was from one such tribe, and it was this hope that had led to her indiscretion when she was freed from Taexalin. What a fool she had been.

'Why did I not lie about my status?' she reproached herself.

Maawan sat silently in the shadows of the Great Hall, reflecting on the journey that had brought her here to Gabrantovices.

After the coup by Venutius, she had sent a message to her mother, secretly arranging to meet up with her a few miles outside of Stanwic; the seat of Cartimandua's kingdom. But Venutius had heard that she still lived, so he'd sent word throughout Brigantium of rewards for her carcass. She travelled under cover by day and night, heading north toward Vindolanda, the place where she believed her father Eachann may still be.

Maawan had covered her head and face with her cape, hoping to find rest for a few hours in the villages and towns of those still supporting Cartimandua. She removed every sign of her royal status, 'cepting the signet ring, given to her by her mother as she fled.

'Take this as proof that you are a goddess, born of a goddess, and a princess of high birth, born of Cartimandua, the High Queen of Brigantia. Let no man recall your illegitimacy, for I have decreed that you will be my heir, and on that you must stand,' the queen had proclaimed, in front of her hand maidens as witnesses, and in the presence of the High Druid of all, Donn Donnlugh.

Maawan stole servant's clothes to delude anyone she might encounter, transforming herself into a servant girl in looks and attitude. Her quick wit and intelligence had carried her far and she was many miles from Stanwic, on a forest-lined route, when she came across the *Braint*. The narrow footpath led past a shrine to Belatucadrus, the god of war, but also the god of humble people. The shrine was constructed of stones surrounding a hollow in the ground. Inside the hollow was a hammered iron bowl, rusted by rain and age. Round the sides of the bowl lay many small items of coins, warrior spearheads, and white feathers from the dove. Families of warriors and war lords leaving for battle would often give a white feather to their men, as a reminder that the gods watched over them in their battles. After victorious battles, feathers were returned to shrines as prayers and gifts of thanksgiving to the gods

Maawan had been worshipping at the shrine when she saw two warriors on horseback approaching. In an instant, she moved toward a snicket of bramble bushes and hid. The horses were covered by blue cloaks with emblems of Venutius showing at the sides. She knew they were her enemies, or at least, enemies of her mother. She watched as the men dismounted, showing spear, dagger and axe under their furs and linen wraps, but displaying bare chest and muscles. They looked fierce and war like as they walked toward the small copse, where the shrine stood. They bowed the knee before the sacred stone shrine. Each took coins from their purse and threw them into the bowl. They made the sign of the Four Fires in the earth around the foot of the shrine, and again bowed with reverence: all this in silence. Maawan moved to shift her stance trying to move further away, but the sound warned of her position. Without a word spoken, the warriors moved in unison to grab Maawan from behind the bushes.

'Ha ha! What 'ave we 'ere?' asked the fatter of the two. His beard was painted red with dye from the woods, and his face was lined with iron pins, around his brows and his nose. The pins had caused his face to look blue, and fearsome. He, like the other, had tattoos covering his upper chest. Pictures of bulls and eagles, of dragons and gods covered each of the Braint. Maawan tried to fight them off, but her punches were lost in the wind.

'Look at this, Locryn. She's a fighter, she is,' laughed the taller of the two, as he grappled to hold her.

'Stop that now. Don't you know you are on holy ground, young 'un?' he asked.

Maawan gave up struggling. 'Leave me alone to worship at the shrine,' she said.

'We will. When you tell us who you are and what you are up to.'

Thinking quickly, Maawan responded. 'I am but a servant girl, who has lost her mistress. My name is Milburga. We were in the woods together and I came across this shrine. I have been calling for my mistress, but she has not come for me. I don't know what to do, but to wait here,' she pleaded.

The two men took to counsel at that point, and grunting some conversation, they turned in unison to look at Maawan. 'You had better come with us then, Milburga. We are going to the Festival of Veteris,' said Locryn. 'It is likely that your mistress will be there. Sit on Thanat's steed, little 'un.'

At that, the tall braint pulled Maawan up onto his horse. They made their way to the grounds of the festival of Veteris. The field was filling with tents and crowds, as the two warriors arrived with Maawan. They found their friends, the rest of the band of highly acclaimed fighters, including Beornbran Byrde, the most notorious of the famous men. These were the ones who it is told, had torn the heads off Roman warriors with their bare hands. Maawan knew that she would share the same fate if they discovered who she was, so she intended on leaving the party as soon as she was able.

'Oh! There is my mistress. She is over by the black tent. I will thank you, sirs and leave you now.' She turned to run toward the tent, but as she turned, she found herself confronted by Taexalin the Wild. She knew him of old, from her stepfather's company, and he recognised her immediately. She ducked to avoid him, but he stood on the hem of her skirts. She ripped the skirt away from him and continued running. Chasing away, she zigzagged round the crowds and the rings, but Taexalin was too quick for her. He grabbed her arm and tripped her leg.

She fell and he was on top of her. The crowds looked on while the wild man groped her.

'Ah! Wench. You know you want me. Here I am.' He rolled round with her until he had a firm grip on her. Dragging her up, he thrashed her round the head, vowing to make her pay for his trouble.

'I deserve the reward money for your deliverance to Venutius,' he shouted. 'It would be more than any money I could make in the ring tonight,' so dragging Maawan with him, he went to get his horse. He added, 'and, my little lady, before taking you to Venutius, I might well enjoy the fruits of your body myself.' Tying Maawan's wrist to his own, he sat her on the horse, wrapped himself tightly round her as he rode off the field and toward the road.

A tear tracked down Maawan's cheek as she sat in the darkness of the Great Hall, shivering with fear. Edric came through the double doors of the lord's house. He went to the wooden carved chest in his mother's room and took out the deep red ceremonial cloak which had belonged to his father. He wrapped it round his frame and pinned it with a clasp bearing the Four Fires of the Brigantes Cross. He stood tall in his new-found confidence and went to join in the revelry outside. As he entered the Great Hall, he saw Maawan hiding in the servant's stall, and called to her.

'Maawan, I want to talk to you. Why are you in here? You should be celebrating with us. Come.' He beckoned her to take his arm and walk with him, but she backed away.

'No. My lord. This is your night, and tonight you must celebrate as you would, were I not here. I will meet you tomorrow when your head has found its shoulders, and we will talk then.'

Her long hair fell softly round her neck like a silken waterfall of red fire shimmering round her face. Her green eyes shone in the candlelight. Edric gazed into the deep pools of emerald, feeling the pull of their enchantment. For a moment he was taken aback, as she held his gaze; but coming to his senses, he stepped away, bowed, and bid her good night.

He left to return to the music and drinking. But in that one moment, Edric knew that this was the woman he wanted to marry.

CHAPTER FOUR

A'LORG
Searching

THE MORNING SHOWED promise of sunshine, but Maawan rose too early to notice. She had decided that she must leave, even before she speaking to Edric. It would be noon before he or the household would wake. She washed and dressed, being careful not to disturb Osma and Yetta, who were wrapped up together in a blanket of horsehair on top of a pile of hay.

Maawan crept out of the house, through the fenced wall of the lord's home, and then scurried down the path toward the outer gate of the settlement. Looking behind her to make sure she was not being followed, she climbed the wooden stairway which led to an escape hole in the outer fence. She knew she would have to jump several feet from this opening, but she could not risk asking the gate keeper to open the gate for her. She looked out of the hole, and down onto the road beyond. Wrapping her cape around her, she fearlessly jumped. As her body met the ground, she rolled into a ball and landed more softly than she had anticipated. She rolled a few yards and then listened before uncurling. Nothing stirred. She stood up, and looking round for the way to go, ran to the forest beyond the houses, and into the dense summer growth. She was gone.

The sun was high in the sky, and people had begun to make their way to the water hole and light their fires in order to make fresh provisions for the day.

Bianna looked round her mother's bedroom, which she had taken as her own. She tried to shake off the deep dreams she'd had. Her head felt heavy, though she had not drunk the wine or beer to any great extent. But she remembered the dream; she had been flying through the air above the sept, as she so often seemed to do in her sleep these days. She had seen the crown of Brigantia falling from the hole high up in the defence wall, above the gateway. She had swooped, like a bird, to catch the crown in her hands. But as she scooped it up, it fell from her fingers and the precious power it held seemed to roll away with it.

She tried to recollect the images that she had encountered in the dream. She tried to fathom the meaning of it all, but she could not. 'I must talk with Dugall,' she thought. 'He will know what to make of it.' A smile spread across her face as she thought about seeing him and talking with him. She hugged herself, giving a little skip, then giggled. But the events of the day before flooded her thoughts again. The things belonging to her dear mother, lying here and there around the room brought a great sadness. A head covering and tie, her skirts, and a shirt top with lace around the sleeves. Her ceremonial bodice made of the softest dyed blue wool, and her shoes, tiny and covered in iron beads were placed carefully over a stool at one end of the room. The huge black cloak lay over the bed for warmth, but Bianna rose and enveloped herself in the smell of it. She walked around the room, shaking off the night, and examining the treasures, choosing which she would wear today. This day. This day of new beginnings.

Bianna got the fire started and soon a brace of pheasants was roasting over a pan collecting the juices. Osma was discussing with Yetta the happenings from the night before. 'Oh! Yetta. My lord, Edric, he was so fine! I am in love with him, and I would throw myself in front of him if only he would marry me,' she giggled.

'Fat chance of that, Osma. He will take a royal bride now, and no mistake. I will have one of his men as my husband. Beored will do for me. He is a fine boy and by the time he is old enough to go through the fire, I will be old enough to have him,' Yetta replied.

Osma screwed her face. 'Ugh! No! I want someone older, with more warrior rewards. I would have one of the braint, if ever I get the chance to meet them.' As the girls discussed their wedding prospects, Osma swept the hall and Yetta gathered the hay from around the stall where they slept. It was at this point that they remembered Maawan.

'Where is Maawan?' asked Osma. 'Her cloak has gone. Is she fetching water? She should be helping us here, and not loitering outside.'

'I haven't seen her all morning,' responded Yetta, showing no interest at all in the missing girl. She continued to gather the stary and rearrange it on the floor of the stall, but Osma was already outside looking for Maawan.

Yetta continued to talk about Beored, who was growing into a handsome young man.

'He is tall and good looking, with a smile and a wit that makes me laugh out loud. I think he likes me, but nothing had passed between us, so I have no way of knowing what Beored thinks of me.' She stopped for a minute to enjoy her thoughts before correcting herself. 'Better get on,' she told herself, and swept up an armful of hay to shake.

At that moment she heard the sound of metal hitting the floor and rolling away. She dropped the hay and began to look under the chaff for the culprit. There, beneath her pillow, was a ring. This, she knew, was no ordinary adornment. It was made of gold, and it wrapped around itself leaving a flat buckle end where the Cross of Brigantia was etched. Hidden on the back of the ring, was a 'wild pony' insignia: a regal symbol. A signet ring of great significance.

Yetta quietly popped it into her skirts and hid it.

In the other room, Edric was dressing. The huge belt that held his father's iron sword was slung on a hook behind the oak door. The sword, honed to warrior keenness, still held its place in the belted scabbard. Edric placed the belt respectfully round his waste and hitched the sword onto his back. He took the dagger, decorated with iron filigree, the finest that could be made. He weighed the dagger in his hand, and then tucked that also in his belt. The cloak he wore last night was strewn across the bed, abandoned after the heavy drinking. Carefully and neatly folding the cloak, Edric laid it with precision across the bed. He walked out of the room, heading toward the village.

It was well into the night before Edric finished visiting all the homes and families in the sept. He was welcomed and praised by his tribe for the killing of Taexalin, for word had got out about the slaying of the wild man, and estimation of Edric's warrior abilities had risen. It was beginning to dawn on him that his life had changed with the passing of his mother, and the more so with his saving of Maawan. As he walked back home, he thought again about her green eyes and wild hair the colour of fiery bracken, and his step quickened.

When he entered the Great Hall, it was in darkness. He did not want to disturb the girls or Maawan, so he went straight to his room. He would talk to Maawan tomorrow, rising early and speaking to her before the fast was broken.

The sun had no intentions of showing itself that morning. The rain came down and the wind blew. But Edric rose early and without dressing, he took the red cloak of his father's and muffled in the comforting warmth, he went to look for Maawan.

As he entered the Great Hall, Osma jumped up. Kicking Yetta awake, she grabbed her bed cover around her and bowed low as Edric approached. 'Where is Maawan?'

'We don't know, *Breehin*. We have not seen her since the night of the high moon.'

'Find her at once, and fetch her to me,' ordered Edric.

Both girls, although barely awake, left the great Hall, searching in the direction of the kitchen scullery and outside, with but a bed cover to hide their almost naked bodies. Edric washed and returned to his room to dress for the day. He had only just belted the sword and dagger in place when shouts came from the outside. Buite dashed in.

'Edric, Lord Edric,' he called. 'There are warriors advancing on the southern road. There are about ten or eleven of them. They bear the standard of Rome. What would you have us do?' Buite was shouting in panic, but Edric remained calm.

'Don't worry Buite. Go to the Druid Grove and ask them to join us. Get the other men to come here. They must bring their weapons. Tell the women and children to hide. All will be well.' Buite followed his chief's orders.

In minutes, the Druids arrived, led by Dugall Dubthach. There were nine of them, all wearing the Druid ceremonial colours depicting their rank. Black or brown cloaks were worn by the serving Druids and workers, of which there were three. Red or blue cloaks were the sign of the warrior Druids; ones who had fought against the enemies alongside the warrior lords and kings. Four of the Druids wore these colours. White cloaks were worn by the priests and seers. Dugall, the principal Druid, wore a white cloak with red lining, depicting his priesthood and warrior achievements. A pin held his cloak at the shoulder in which he had fastened a spray of mead wort and rowan.

His acolyte, the bearded Maccar, wore a white cloak with a lining of blue. Though a good ten years older than Dugall, Maccar was happy to serve him. Both men were of noble caste; their bearing spoke of authority and loyalty. Each Druid took a stool and placed it in a circle round the fire in Edric's house. They sat silently, facing the fire. Each held in his left hand a fey of judgement, and in his right hand, a staff. Dugall offered a stool to Bianna, placing her in the circle with the Druids, by his side, as a sign of her advancement in the Druid order. Her brother, noticing this advancement, smiled, and nodded. Bianna shuffled a little on the stool and nodded back. Edric stood at the door of the house, waiting. As the fighting men and warriors arrived, Edric spoke loudly enough to be heard by them all as they gathered outside the lord's great house.

'We don't know the reason for this visit, but we must be ready…ready to meet them in friendship, or in battle. The Druid's will give us their judgement, and we will act upon it. Hide where you can, and at my word, surround them and take them. Now go and be ready. My own men, go to the gate and when the troop arrives, enquire as to their purpose.' Buite, Beored, Cerdic, Bryth, and the others ran off with sword and spear in hand, toward the outer gate. Edric stood his ground and waited.

As the band of Roman soldiers approached, Beored called out to them. 'Hail. Come you in peace to Gabrantovice, Roman brothers?'

One from their band called out, 'We are searching for one called 'The Wild One.' He has consorted with the enemy of Rome, and we have orders to bring him before our governor, Scapula, and your queen, Cartimandua. Can you help us in our quest?'

'Will you lay down your arms in order to gain entry to our sept?' asked Beored.

'We will. If you have information that can help us.'

'My Lord Edric Beornraed, Lord Bloodeworthe of Gabrantovice, may be able to help you. It was he that did slay Taexalin some nights ago.'

'We would like to parley with your lord, if we may.'

Cerdic ran back to Edric to inform him of the conversation with the soldiers, and Edric looked at the Druid circle and waited for a judgement. One of the company threw spice powder into the fire, and it sparked and cracked while a cloud of smoke spread inside the circle. One by one the Druids began to chant.

When boar and eagle meet
At the brown and the boar seat,
Though death and loss lay hand in hand
Our soul torn in a thousand strands,
Yet still, the god of fire will rise
Reshaping the demise,
Revealing embers of the soul.
Reclaiming ruins; making whole.'

As the chant continued, Dubthach turned and knelt before Bianna, and spoke directly to her, as if trying to convey some deeper meaning in his words. He spoke softly but urgently, prophesying, 'The time is coming when the gods call to the four winds, and to the fire, and the High One will return.' He held her gaze for a moment before turning to Edric to pronounce the judgement.

'Let them in and tell them of your victory over Taexalin. But do not tell them of your interest in Venutius. For the sake of your people, respect Cartimandua this day.'

And so, the word was given to let the Romans in. The Decurion were brought before Edric who welcomed them as the Lord *Breehin*. They did not bow before him, as they saw themselves as the higher order, but they gave a salute, touching their right fist against their left shoulder, in a sign of respect. 'In the name of Governor Scapula and Queen Cartimandua, we bring greetings,' said the one who seemed to be the leader. He eyed Edric up and down, taking in the youth and stature of the warrior before him. Edric did the same, making mental note of the armour, weaponry, and stance of the men in front of him. He knew he must not display any facial expression that would betray his hatred.

'Welcome,' he lied.

'Is it true that you slaughtered Taexalin the Wild?' the Roman asked.

'Yes. I did,' answered Edric. 'My men were witness to that fact.' Buite and Beored moved forward to show themselves and nodded their heads in affirmation.

'Have you further proof, lord, of this action? We must be clear on this matter before we return to our master.'

At this Edric took out from his belt the talisman that he had ripped from the neck of Taexalin and swung it in the air. 'I have proof enough. He is dead, and good riddance,' he said. A ripple of approval went round the soldiers.

'That is good news,' said the Roman leader. 'I have one more question for you, lord. Was he travelling alone when you came upon him?'

Edric thought fast. 'Yes,' he lied. 'He was alone.' He didn't know why he had done that, except that the face of Maawan flashed in front of his eyes, and he wanted her to be as far removed from any trouble as possible.

'Then we will thank you, lord, and take our leave.' At this, the Roman warriors left, satisfied of the death of Taexalin. But Edric was troubled. As soon as the soldiers had left the area, Edric called together his fighting men.

'We have a job to do,' he told them.

The company of young warriors set out the following day, before the sun had broken the sky, disguised as marauders, but with warrior swords concealed across their backs. Edric had spoken of the need to find Maawan before anyone else did, and to bring her back to safety at Gabrantovice. They planned a venture to find her, and the troop of

Romans who visited them the day before.

They were driven to kill the group of ten enemies before they had chance to leave the area, but not wanting to bring condemnation onto the people of Gabrantovices should any escape, they determined to carry out the execution under cover, posing as wanderers and vagabonds.

A good ride later, the young lord and his men saw the flicker of flames rising from the Roman campfire. A little way off they took stock of the situation, weighing up how best to secure their cause. They knew that surprise was on their side. So many times before, Edric had used stealth to surprise his prey, though he had only used this tactic on other Brigantine tribes to make their lives uncomfortable. This time he used his experience to surprise the troop of soldiers before they could get to their weapons. Edric directed five of his men to the left, and four to the right to surround the camp. They dismounted before they reached the camp and silently drew their swords. They took a man each, slicing into his throat, or puncturing his heart. Silently, they took the chains and weapons from each body and silently walked away from the bodies. Once they were on horseback again, they made the sign of offering to Taranis, the god who required sacrifices, and rode away.

That night, as they made camp several miles away from the death camp and Gabrantovices, they allowed themselves to celebrate. They sang songs of victory over the enemy, and battle songs of old. Into the night they celebrated, until one by one they fell asleep. Except Edric. Edric could not sleep, for Maawan beckoned him.

CHAPTER FIVE

ELLESTOB
Veiled Place

AAWAN RAN NORTHWARDS, watching the sun to give her direction as she travelled. The forest was dense and sometimes it was hard for her to see through the thick treetops to know where the sun was, but it created glimmers of shadows, enough to give her a fair indication of the way to go.

She followed the sun for three days, sleeping in a cave one night and in a rocky outcrop the next. She avoided the hamlets of two or three houses at Brotton and Marske, even though she felt tempted to ask for food and shelter for the night. She had not yet put enough distance between herself and Gabrantovices, and remained too near to Edric, for she still felt his breath on her face.

That night she cradled in a hollow underneath one of the old oaks and wrapped her cloak around her. The weather was clement, and she slept for some hours without concern. As morning called to the sunbeams and the birdsong began calling the day to awake, Maawan stirred from her sleep. She knew that today she must find shelter and food before she could continue her journey; so set out with renewed purpose, trying to ignore her hunger. As she travelled, a stream bubbling through the trees and meandering through rocks and mossy ground gave her a cool drink and a place to soothe her blistered feet. Three days of running and walking had shown their consequence. Her determination to reach Vindolanda was sustained by the need to protect herself from supporters of Venutius and the renegade Brigantine tribes.

Maawan decided that the next place she came to would be her resting place for a while. She stopped for a moment at the top of a low hill to take in the landscape. She had left the forest and had been moving toward moorland. The widening scape gave her little shelter and no sense of obscurity unless she crawled on her hands and knees in the bracken and heather. Watching for the sun to show her bearings, she altered her course a little to the west and continued until she came upon Ellestob.

Ellestob was a small hamlet of about twelve roundhouses, bearing few constructed security measures. The village had no outer defence wall, only a storm barrier. Outside the barrier, a stream ran almost completely round the outer edges. A dam had been built were the stream tapered off, so that the sept seemed to be in the middle of the water, like an island. A narrow, single bridgeway across the water led into the village. This created a sufficient barrier for defences, and warning of approaching visitors. The open field area outside the water barrier had sheep pens, so Maawan guessed that these people were farmers and had little time for fighting. She moved openly toward the walkway and entered. An old woman sat by the path. Her head was covered with a dirty scarf, but her warty face was exposed. Her teeth were missing, so when she smiled it looked like her tongue was falling out of her mouth, as it had no bars to keep it in. But smile she did as Maawan approached.

'Hey ho, merry wench. Welcome to Ellestob, home to travellers, jugglers, and *scates*. Enter here and find peace,' she said. Maawan had trouble understanding the old woman's speech because of her excess of tongue, which sprayed saliva like a fountain. To avoid the spray, she bobbed her head in acknowledgement and walked by. 'A coin for an old seer?' called the woman.

'I have nothing,' responded Maawan.

'Then you'll be needin' me 'elp, young 'un.'

'Indeed. I may well,' she answered.

''elp me up then, and I'll see thee right.' As she began to stand, Maawan turned to give her a hand, pulling her upright. The old woman leaned into Maawan's ear, and with a spray of slobber, whispered, 'Be careful who follows. Be careful who you sit with, for I see a dark shadow over your shoulder.'

Maawan wiped the spray from around her ear as the old woman walked toward the group of huts huddled together in a circle, beckoning Maawan to follow her. There was no-one to be seen, so Maawan surmised that the people might be working in some nearby fields. Doors made from elder twigs and branches woven together in frames were pushed across some of the openings. These would give little protection when there was need of a weather shield, or worse, Maawan thought.

A ring made up of benches had been laid out in the centre of the small hut-like homes of the villagers. In the centre of the ring was a sacred Mother Elder; queen of trees, planted for healing and protection of the people of Ellestob. Maawan silently followed the old hag through a gap in the benches into the middle of the opening, taking care to circle the magical tree. They walked to the other end and sat on one of the top benches. Soon, Maawan noticed a face or two peeping out of the doorways, looking at her. Other faces appeared from behind the huts; and then, one by one, children appeared. They came into the circle of benches, and without saying a word, sat down cross legged before the visitor. They stared at Maawan until she began to fidget under their scrutiny. It wasn't long before the children began to talk and play in front of her. 'Oh,' she thought, 'I'm sitting in the children's ring.' She smiled and began to engage with them, asking their names, and making small jokes with them. A girl of about eight and a boy a little older asked her name. Maawan, anxious to remain anonymous until she knew the status of the villagers, answered with the story she had told the Braint.

'My name is Milburga,' she lied.

A little later, the mothers, women, and older girls began to come out of the houses and join in the conversation. There were about twenty-five of them, and Maawan wondered how the village catered for all these folk. Each woman had a shawl of woven linen in varying shades of blue, purple, and green; and they looked clean and well fed.

'It's not very often we get travellers here,' one said.

'Have you come far?' asked another.

Maawan stuck to her story about losing her mistress who was travelling northward. She added that her mistress had two companions: war lords for Cartimandua. Maawan waited and watched for a reaction to this statement. A low hush resonated round the benches. The women looked from one to the other assessing what this news meant to them.

'Cartimandua? Is she travelling with them?' they asked, looking from one to the other in general excitement.

'Will she be coming along the same route?'

'Will they be calling here?'

The questions came furiously, like shots from ten different slings. Maawan answered each one as she could without causing anxiety to these women, and not wanting her fabrications to cause consternation.

'My mistress rides with war lords, there only to guide and protect her as she goes to meet her family in the north. I know nothing about the queen. But I do not know how to find my mistress. On the road we were beset by four barbarians who caused us to scatter. I ran for my life but lost my way. I do not know who the raiders were, but I did notice they wore a sign on their forearm, which looked like 'Venti',' she said. Maawan drew the sign of wind in the ground in front of her, hoping for a clue to their affiliations. A gasp went round the benches, as the women digested this information. A buxom woman came forward and seemed to take charge. She folded her arms to rest them across her large belly, hidden under her ample skirts. Her voice was soft and reassuring, as a mother talking to her children.

'Shush,' she said, patting the air down as a gesture for quiet. 'If these marauders are Venutius' men, then we must warn our husbands and families of their nearness. We are the queen's people and will not be unprepared in defending ourselves against her treacherous husband.' At this, Maawan signed with relief. Meanwhile, the women darted backwards and forwards into their homes and into the fields a little way out, shouting for their husbands, fathers, and sons to return quickly.

Camulo was the first to return from the field. He sent for 'Milburga' to join him in his home. "I am chief of these people,' he explained to her, pointing with an open palm to indicate the homes beyond his doorway. His face wore a broad grin as he introduced himself.

'I am Camulo.'

Maawan knew that the Brigantes carefully chose the names of their children, each having a special prophetic meaning. Camulo meant 'Champion,' and so he was. Arranged in his house were the trophies and rewards he had received from victorious battles and encounters. This was no ordinary man. Maawan knew she needed to be careful not to let her story escalate: she knew of men like this who would think nothing of seeking out the 'raiders' and cutting their throats. But Maawan wanted to rest, so she determined to make light of the incident she had fabricated, and hopefully get something to eat and a bed for the night

Camulo questioned her for a while, and each question he asked, Maawan spoke of the queen, or the Romans, or Rome, or the Scots. She spoke with innocence, as any servant girl might.

'I know very little, lord, except for conversations overheard. I am told that the Roman soldiers are numerous and have already taken the south of Albion. Every day, their borders are extended. I know some are fearful of them, and the changes they may bring to our lands. There are stories I have heard of the Romans slaughtering whole families in the name of their gods, but our queen is a wise queen, I am led to believe. Her accord with Emperor Claudius was only to save lives. She is doing all she can to make Brigantia safe and secure.' After further questioning by Camulo, Maawan revealed the extent of her fear of Venutius. 'I have heard of his hatred for the Romans, and how he plots against our queen. I do not understand how someone can turn against their spouse and want to bring about their end. I do not know whom I should fear most; him or the invading army'

'Fear only your own thoughts, Maawan. I have found that fear can stint courage, and courage is what we need in these times. As for the queen and Venutius, well, I think their marriage is unquestionably over. Time will show how the heart of Brigantia will continue to beat.'

Eventually Camulo turned his attention to his stomach, shouting for food and beer. He ordered Maawan to remain with him. The buxom woman who earlier that day had taken charge, came into the chief's house holding a platter. She bobbed in respect as she entered the roundhouse, her bosom bobbing with her as she leaned forward. She introduced herself as Raegan, the wife of Camulo. The platter she carried bore slices of roast lamb and ham, with beets and potatoes, alongside several different cheeses, flat breads, and biscuits. Raegan placed the platter on the table with three wooden tankards which she filled with ale. Raegan sat with her husband, sharing bread and the platter with Maawan. She had an easy, relaxed way about her. Maawan liked her and found it easy to relax also. At least for a while, she dropped her guard and enjoyed the food.

'You will stay with us tonight, Milburga,' said Raegan, 'and tomorrow we will talk some more of your mistress, and how we might help you to find her.'

'I am grateful for your hospitality,' Maawan responded, giving a nod of thanks to Camulo and his wife.

'There is room for you to bed by the side stall, with enough hay for comfort.'

Maawan settled down that night feeling warm and safe. She slid easily into sleep, promising herself that she would reward these good people, when she had the opportunity.

That night Maawan dreamed of Venutius. Tentacles grew from his shoulders, waving and winding themselves round, moving like the wind, reaching for her. The Warlord of Brigantia moved toward her, wrapping his tendrils around her throat, choking the breath out of her soul. From nowhere, the sound of mighty hooves at full gallop resonated in a flash. Maawan tried to shout out to the rider, but the sound struggled feebly to leave her lips. A muffled 'Help...' escaped, as the horse and rider materialised. The beautiful black steed charged; its rider expertly cutting and slicing off the vaporous tendrils of her antagonist. She was freed.

She awoke the next morning with Edric on her mind.

The dream caused her to feel confused. Her enemy was Venutius: he had ordered her execution. But her feelings for Edric, also an enemy of her mother, left her bewildered. She remembered the night he had saved her from Taexalin, and how she had been so grateful to him. But his words of revenge against her family and the Romans weighed heavy on her mind. His disdain for her mother's alliance with the invaders seemed deep rooted. Maawan could see only the good in her mother, and her desire to keep her people safe from battle. Yes, when Cartimandua aligned herself with the invaders, they paid her well for the privilege. She had promised to make improvements to the lives of her people with the spoils of this alliance. She had procured peace between them and Brigantia — peace that was jeopardised only because of fools like Edric, who would not bend the knee to the Roman conquerors.

'So why,' Maawan reasoned with herself, 'do I not feel anger toward Edric, as I should?'

She rose and washed in the stream flowing beside the sheep pens then went looking for Raegan. Raegan and Camulo were already enjoying breaking the night's fast. The table was set with all sorts of fruits and cakes. Raegan beckoned Maawan to join them.

'Sit here, my dear, and enjoy these fresh fruits from the orchard. I baked the cakes myself, and there is fresh milk from the goats. Drink. It will make you strong for your travels,' she said. Maawan sat opposite the couple and helped herself to the milk and cakes. She realised that the little hamlet was in many ways, a wealthy one. She asked Camulo about his trophies displayed round the walls, showing interest in these loyal subjects of the queen.

'Have you fought in many battles, lord?' she asked.

'Indeed. I fought against the insurgentem from Rome, at first, but realised that our queen is right to stand with them. Battle is unnecessary and losing one's life for something that is inevitable is foolishness of the highest order.' He continued, 'When the path is dark and holds no hope, then you must look for the light. Peace comes in the morning, and here we have had peace for four harvests.' He got up and walked round the room, pointing to one trophy after the other.

'This I won for standing with my lady, the queen, against the treacherous Brigante who would kill their own people rather than look to peace.' He pointed to a sack of leather, placing his hand inside and taking out coins and gold rings. Trailing them through his fingers and back into the sack, he grinned. Pointing to another he continued. 'This one I won for killing two boars with my own hands, to save a young lad trapped by them.' He tapped the heads of the boars which had been stuffed and mounted on boards. Their tusks held decorations of chains and amulets, as if they had been made for that sole purpose. 'And this one,' pointing to an iron neck chain, 'I won for having the head of a bandit who would have had mine, had I not been as quick.' He appeared indifferent to these testimonials of his warrior prowess, but the wall told the true story. This champion was a hard fighting man: one to whom Maawan would have been delighted to give position in her protectorate, should the need arise.

Camulo sat again, picking up his knife and stabbing an apple with gusto. He ate it from the knife, wiping the juice from his mouth with his sleeve. His wife looked on with pride. She knew she had a good husband: one who, though sometimes hard, was always fair. Changing the subject of her husband's warrior triumphs, she asked, 'So, what with you, little one? Where will you venture next? Will you look for your mistress? If so, we may be able to help.'

Maawan was thoughtful. 'If it pleases you, I would like to stay here for a while before moving on. My mistress will be far gone now, so I must follow by my own devices. She was travelling northward, and I will continue on that route. But I would like to stay, maybe work, and earn some provisions for my journey before I leave.'

'Yes,' answered Raegan without hesitation. 'You can help with the children and tending the goats. In exchange, we have a pony and a sack that can be filled with whatever we have when you are ready to move on. Is that acceptable to you?'

Maawan was more than pleased with this, though she had never dealt with goats before. But she was determined to learn all she could as she made this journey to safety. She was pleased with the safe haven of Ellestob. A few days delay would not hinder her plan.

In fact, she settled into the village way of life very easily. She loved the children, and discovered she had a natural way with them. They loved her, calling her '*Grainne* Milbu' as a sign of their affection. She played with them endlessly each day, making up games to amuse them. Some games she invented to get them into the stream and wash more often, and other games to help the farm hands picking the harvest. The workers and old men alike joked and laughed with her. Those summer days were filled with bright sunshine and laughter. Things became fun for the children, and without realising it, Maawan taught them many new ways of living.

'Have you noticed the way Milburga brings such warmth and love to our sept, Camulo? asked Reagan one day, as they watched the antics of the children playing and singing with her.

'I have indeed, wife. She reminds me so much of one other from long ago,' he reminisced.

Maawan carefully learned to tend the goats too, and the goat-hand became a friend in but a few days. When his goats increased milk flow, he could not help but grin.

'I know the blessing comes through your gentle milking,' he told her.

She tended the beehives, and that summer the honey increased three-fold. The apple orchard yielded abundance when Maawan touched the trees. The central Elder flowered profusely and when it was fully in blossom; it seemed as if the tree was lit by millions of little lights. It was a place where the fairie folk danced, and the good people of Ellestob made wine from the exceptional blooms. It seemed that Maawan had had about her a fairie enchantment that created a profusion of abundance wherever she went. It seemed that everything she did in the sept was blessed. Her warmth won the villagers hearts and when Maawan decided it was time to move on before winter set in, a spirit of heaviness settled on the people.

Camulo led the pony out of the stall by the harvest store. The children had helped pack the pony, loading her with bread, cheeses, apples, and a water skin. There was a blanket over her back, and another rolled up and fastened to her stocky rear. The women of the village came out with a gift they had made for Maawan: a double-lined red cloak, woven from finely spun flax. Each woman had designed their own family pattern, painting them with blacks and blue dyes onto the sections of the cloak. They told Maawan she would need the warmth, now the days were getting shorter and the nights colder. Raegan came last to wish Maawan 'god-speed,' giving her an iron pin to hold the cloak in place. She hugged Maawan to her breast as if she was her own daughter, almost smothering her in the midst.

'This belonged to my father, Milburga. I want you to have it, in thanks for all the joy you have brought to our village.'

When Raegan curtseyed, Maawan wondered if the people perceived the nobility that she had tried to hide. Maawan looked round for Camulo but did not see him.

'Where is Camulo?' she asked. 'I want to say goodbye to him, also.'

The villagers laughed and pointed behind her. Sitting on a magnificent chestnut stallion, in full warrior colours and wearing a helmet decorated with ram's horns, was Camulo.

'I am at your service, my lady, for as long as you need me,' he said, bowing low from his high position. Maawan almost rejected the offer but thought better of it. She had come to realise that this companion would not be deterred, once having made his decision. She bowed in thanks and mounted the pony, Camulo taking the lead. The villagers waved and shouted their good wishes, until Maawan could hear them no longer.

That night, Camulo made camp by a stream on the north side of the hills. The fire comforted them as they took bread. Camulo took an apple and rolled it round in his hand as if he was about to play ball. Maawan enquired some more of the champion and his history. He reminisced about days gone by; of his youth and how he had met the High Queen of Brigantia. At this Maawan tried to hide her excitement.

'You have actually met Cartimandua? How? Please tell,' she begged him.

'I was her guard in the days before her marriage to Venutius. I was her most trusted champion. It was through me that she met my most loyal friend Eachann Beli Mawr. We were warriors together when the Roman army first landed on our shores. Claudius of Rome was our enemy, and we fought together, killing many of their men.'

'Tell me of Eachann. I have heard the name before.' Maawan tried to suppress her eagerness on hearing mention of her father. Even his name made her hungry for information. His name was all she knew of him.

'Eachann was the champion of Carvetti. He was the Fair Shining Slayer, known as Beli Mawr, a warrior of great ability, with many trophies. Venutius was Carvetti High Lord when Queen Cartimandua asked for his help against the Romans. They made an alliance; but Venutius would not leave Carvetti at that time. He sent Eachann to the queen in his stead.'

'Is that when Eachann met the queen?'

'The moment their eyes settled on each other; they were insane with passion. Eachann sealed their love with a ring. To this day, I doubt that the queen has removed it. They were inseparable and would have married, had it not been for Venutius. When he heard of the lovers, he was worried for his own position, so he determined to get rid of

Eachann. But not before Eachann had made the queen pregnant. They had twin daughters, and ten months later had another daughter.

'What happened to the daughters?'

Camulo went on, enjoying the reminiscing as he reached for his knife.

'It is told that the three were born of a Fairie King, and that they themselves were Fairie children. I cannot say if this is true, for Eachann, although praised as a god for his fighting prowess, was as human as you or I. The twins were slaughtered by Venutius only last year, and the youngest daughter—Maawan, has disappeared. She would be about your age now.' Camulo looked at Maawan and nodded. 'Yes, she would be about your age. About sixteen or seventeen, I would say. Her hair is the same colour, too.'

When Camulo spoke of her sisters, Maawan closed her eyes and covered them with her hands. Her mind invoked memories she had not dared to touch since hearing of their slaughter, nor dared allow her heart to grieve. Taken by surprise, she felt the enormous loss for the first time. Unable to contain her sadness, she allowed the tears to flow; raw sobs from the depth of her soul ran down her face and into her hands. Camulo moved to comfort her. He wrapped his strong arm around her.

'There is no shame in crying, little one,' he said. He did not ask why she wept but remained silent for a good while. Gently he freed his hands from comforting Maawan, and taking his knife up again, he continued to slice the apple, as if what he was about to say wasn't important. He tried to hide his agitation, but Maawan detected the nervous flick of the apple skin that showed he was troubled.

'Venutius is still searching for her. There is a ransom on her head,' he said.

Maawan wanted to touch his hand; bring peace to his agitation.

'But where were you, Camulo, while the queen was with Eachann?' Maawan continued, eager to know every detail of her early life.

'I was by my lady's side. I was there when the lovers met; I watched as they fell in love, and then rejoiced with them as their children grew. I watched until Venutius arrived and Eachann escaped his murderous intent. The queen did not love Venutius. But for the sake of her people, she had no choice but to join in marriage with that murderer.'

Maawan sat silently for a while, taking in all the detail of the story being told. Camulo cut at the apple; he ate a slice, then continued. 'It was at that time that Raegan came into my life. The queen needed someone to take the children to safety. Along with the High Druid, I took the children to Raegan. Raegan hid them away for almost three years, until the queen, married to Venutius, held a stronger position, and could safely call them back. During those days, I was protector of the princesses, and it was then that I took Raegan as my wife. We have been together ever since.' His eyes smiled along with his heart, as he thought about his beloved wife. 'When the union between Cartimandua and Claudius of Rome was established, my work was done. I returned the children to her and asked permission to continue my life in the place of my birth. With her permission, Raegan and I travelled back home to Ellestob.'

Camulo looked at Maawan with tenderness, but with a tired expression. 'Milburga, it is time to rest now. Ask me no more questions tonight.'

'Lord, may I know one more thing?' Maawan knew she would not rest until she knew about her father. 'May I ask about Eachann? Does he still live?'

'Little one, he lives with the gods now. He has gone to the Fire of Mars Belatucadrus from whence he came. He is immortal.'

Maawan knew she could ask no more of Camulo this night. Sadness came upon her as a wave on the beach, and once touching her, until she felt the cold dampness of the night washing over her as a grief she had never experienced, nor anticipated.

CHAPTER SIX

CEITHIR GAOTHAN
The Four Winds

EDRIC HAD RETURNED home after the raid and slaughter of the Decurion, but immediately ordered a search for Maawan. He marched restlessly about the sept, shouting orders to any man he saw. 'Prepare to leave,' he shouted.

Bianna ran after him. 'Edric, let us talk. Edric, you have only just returned. Give your men time to rest. And the horses will need to rest too,' begged Bianna. 'Another moon turn will not impact on your urgency. Give space, I beg of you.'

'I am ready, and my men will be also. We must leave while the fight is in us; while the juices flow,' he spat back. Waving her concerns to the air, he made to leave, marching toward the grove, and calling for the Druids as he went. 'We will be on our way in two days,' he shouted.

He sent three groups of five of his best men southward, east, and west, covering all the territory within five days of Gabrantovices, giving his men orders to sweep wide, and to visit as many of the tribal septs as possible. He and four others travelled northward. But it was as if Maawan had disappeared, for wherever they looked, no one had seen or heard of her.

Edric's obsession with Maawan worried his men; he talked continuously about her, almost obsessing about her hair and eyes; about how he needed to find her and protect her. The men asked questions, both directly to Edric and among themselves.

'Why is this so important to Edric?' they asked Buite, one evening as they camped.

'I don't know,' answered Buite, 'he seems burned up with passion.'

'It seems so senseless to me,' another commented. 'If we were out to fight against our enemies, then I can understand the urgency, but for a woman?'

'He could have any woman he fancies,' said another. The rumblings continued.

Buite and Beored sat with Edric for a while. 'Edric, the men are asking after our objective. Can you give us an idea of the importance of the venture?'

Edric thought for a while before answering. 'My good friends, if I could explain what drives me, I would tell you. But it is as if the gods drive me onwards and toward her. Something inside me drives me to her with a desperation I cannot explain. One day, the gods may reveal why I must find her, but for now, I ask for your obedience. Will you give it to me?'

Even though the men saw the venture as unnecessary, nonetheless, his men obeyed, grateful for the change in daily life and glad of a chance to see a wider world.

On the third day of travel, the company came close to the hamlet of Ellestob. Edric scanned the area from a vantage point high up on the moors. The land opened up in front of him, but he saw no sign of life; no sign of anything other than a stretch of water reflecting the sun.

'Can you see anything Buite?' he asked.

'I see what looks like a river, maybe. The sun makes it difficult to see. There seems to be land shrouded in a heavy mist in the middle. Maybe an island. Maybe not.'

Edric was dazzled by the low sun as he scanned the open moor.

'Nothing here. Let's push on,' he said as he turned his horse away from Ellestob.

The days of searching made Edric weary. Each night they made the camp. The men hunted and fished where they could, but food was short. When opportunity presented itself, they approached some tribal groups, asking for shelter and warmth. On the seventeenth day of travel, they reached the very northern border of their land, with still no sight of Maawan. As they approached a river overlooking Luguvalium, they came upon a shrine to Belisamma, the goddess of water. Each warrior placed an offering on the shrine: a trophy from a dead bandit, a leaf or a flower, or a coloured pebble. All were proffered as thanks for the continuing gift of water.

Edric prayed at the shrine. His hands trembled as he brought a bronze brooch from his small waist pouch. It had been his father's pin; a treasured token. Kissing the breastpin, Edric laid it by the side of the shrine. A tear tracked down his cheek as he offered it to Belisamma. He kneeled, lifting his head to look skyward.

'I am asking for your help, oh! Belisamma, great source of life,' he pleaded. 'If it pleases you, accept my offering and show me where Maawan is hidden. Bring me peace in this, I beg.' He sat at the edge of the river, unbuckling his sword belt. It had rained almost constantly for several days, so everything around him was heavy with water. His heart too was heavy. He was thinking of home, feeling tired and disappointed with the journey. He wondered if his mission would ever be successful. A sinking feeling came over him as he allowed despair to enter his thoughts.

He didn't notice the young girl swimming in the river. She swam nearer to him, almost touching his foot before he realised that she was there, and that she was struggling to breathe. She gasped for air as she plunged under the current. Once, as her head showed above the water, she tried to shout for help; but the sound of the water rushing by silenced her cry. Roused from his melancholy, Edric dived into the icy water without hesitation. The girl slipped through his fingers like an eel, touching him; one moment clinging to his neck as if for her life, and the next, singing a haunting melody in his ear. She swam round him, and as she circled in the water, her carrageen hair, like octopus tendrils, clung to him; wrapping each strand round his arms, then body, then neck. Edric fought the nymph but felt his strength draining. Her song made him sleepy. His thoughts began to embrace the Naiad. He allowed her to take him deeper into the river, each moment taking him nearer to her home. He heard shouting above, but it was too late. The water nymph had him, and he didn't care.

Bryth called out, 'Edric. Edric!' as he ripped off his belt and jumped in the water. He called to the others for help. They ran to the riverbank. Cerdic, realising what was happening as Bryth jumped in, followed in behind him. They swam to where Edric was last seen, and without hesitation dived into the depth of the river. Several minutes seemed to pass.

All three emerged, gasping as they reached the air, encircled by white foam. Edric, flanked by Bryth and Cerdic, reached the safety of the riverbank. He clasped the shoulders of his rescuers, a gesture of gratitude for the bravery that had undoubtedly saved his life.

The nights were drawing in earlier, and autumn changed the shape of the land. Soon it would be Samheim, and Edric knew he must return home for the festival. His people would expect him to lead them in the traditions. This festival marked the end of the harvest season and beginning of the "darker-half" of the year. On this night, the Druids lit a bonfire and gave prayers of celebration for ancestors, a communion with the dead. Edric had to be there.

So it was that on the thirty first day of searching, as the moon changed its phase, the men changed direction and headed south; home. Just three days away from Gabrantovices, the group fell in with the West riders and East riders. They settled a camp for the night and waited for the South riders to join them before travelling the rest of the journey home together. There was a good spirit among the men as they told their travel tales. Biticus was the first to report to Edric.

'We travelled east, Edric, as you ordered, reaching the border of Brigantia where the road leads to Eboracum. There are rumours of Roman digging, stripping our lands of iron and gold. We came upon some bandits, who attacked us. But their attempt at stealing our horses ended swiftly with the bodies of the attackers hanging from the oaks, and their heads severed as trophies to take home. We travelled along the border for twelve days. At every hamlet, village, and sept we stopped and asked after your desire. No one had seen or heard anything about Maawan, 'cept for her name. We were told several times that Maawan is the name of the daughter of Carti. We had to explain that this Maawan was but a servant girl, with no high blood.' He laughed as he told the story. Looking round the group of men, he laughed more.

'Maawan the princess,' indeed! Ha! Though why you, Edric, my lord, should be bothered with her, when you can have any woman you desire, is beyond my understanding.' He laughed again heartily, and the men joined in. The men had been away for almost forty days, yet their humour was light. Notwithstanding, they all knew they would be glad to get home to their families and to see the Northern Sea.

Beored and Wulfnud's team had gone west. They had come across a band of warriors. 'They were our brothers; the Setanti,' explained Beored. 'We spent some time in their camp, asking after your purpose, but they had nothing to give us. Except to tell of the situation in Deva, where the wealth is unimaginable. Copper, tin, lead, gold, and silver is abundant. The filthy Romans want their hands on it, but the Setanti have been fighting them off. Up to four hundred of the alien forces lay dead in the rivers and hills thanks to our brothers.'

Wulfnud was eager to share his knowledge of the situation. 'We stayed and fought with them. They are like madmen when it comes to swords and staff. The foreign scum will never subdue our brothers. The cudgels of their foot soldiers have little chance against the dagger and sword of the Brigante and the Setanti,' he reported, with pride.

'You are good warriors, and I expect nothing less from you, brothers,' endorsed Edric. 'But what of Maawan? Was there any news?'

'No, lord. Nothing! She is gone, like snow on a warm day. Or the moon, as it disappears from our sky each cycle. We saw and heard nothing, lord.'

Edric weighed this and realised that maybe Maawan did not want to be found. He remembered that the Brigante were known to the Romans as 'The Hidden People.' His tribe was exceptional at transforming themselves into shadows.

'Maybe Maawan has this ability,' Edric wondered.

They spent the next hours discussing their travels, feeling that they now had a bigger picture of the invading army: where the Roman soldiers were concentrating their battle strategies and where the Brigante tribes were flourishing. 'I heard rumours of the invader's plans to build a fort at Deva, so that is an area to be watched. If a Roman fort was built there, then the Romans would have a base for taking the west and defending their position from Brigantines in the north.' declared Wulfnud.

Much discussion surrounded this possible objective, and the danger it could present to the Druid grove on Ynys Môn, the sacred place, and the largest training school for the old religion. 'Claudius thinks his campaign warranted, as their need for our metals, ore, and copper is great. And that Druids stand in way of his desire for total occupation of Albion. That the Druidic practices of live sacrifices are barbaric,' added Beored. 'He won't be happy until all the Druids are gone. Dead. No more.'

They ate the remaining food and drank a hefty beer, which Wulfnud had continued his horse pack, for most of the last forty miles. They slept heavily that night, with songs of home on their minds and in their dreams.

Several days passed before Cail and Callan arrived back with the riders from the south. They looked travel-weary, but in good spirits.

'We travelled for five days, deciding to ride the southern border before circling round. We arrived at the border with the Cortiavi and rode the length of it, making headway east. The people there are mostly farmers. Most of the warriors left the septs when the Romans took over a few years ago. The land was filled with the occupiers, setting up their own homes in the middle of our septs and villages. The Cortiavi have accepted defeat, and, like our queen, have taken on the mantle of ally. It makes me sick,' reported Callan. He spat on the ground to show his disgust for the Roman trespassers. 'And...' he began, as if thinking about the value of the information he was about to give. 'We met on the ride, someone who seemed to know you, Edric. He had a voice that spoke as our tongue, but he was riding with four Romans. When they asked where we were from, he seemed to know already, as if he recognised us. 'Ah! Your leader: Edric the Arrogant,' he said, 'How fares he?' We answered carefully, for his manner was aggressive.'

'Did you find out who he was, and where he was going? What did he look like? Was he fair or dark? Was he tall?'

'It is hard to judge a man's height when he is sitting on a horse, but his hands looked small. He wore a hood and hid most of his face. I am afraid we did not find anything more. Cail decided that he didn't like the man or his companions. A fight broke out, in which we slaughtered two of the Romans, but the others fled.' Edric pondered on this, then dropped the thought from his mind.

'We circled back, travelling the southern areas of our own fair land, taking in The Rig, where Venutius built the defence against the Romans, should they invade.' He laughed sarcastically. 'That worked! The whole of the Cortiavi have given in to them.'

'But not us, Callan. Not us. We killed a few unsuspecting Romans for good measure. Got a few trophies too!' smirked Cail. 'And from there we travelled back again, eastward, zig-zagging across Brigantium.'

They continued their report of skirmishes between soldiers, 'Traitors to Brigantia,' and fellow warriors; mostly for the fun of it. But in all this, they were unable to report to Edric that they had seen or heard of Maawan. The following day, they cleared camp and made their way home.

As soon as the warriors were spotted, the gates of Gabrantovices were opened and the people came to welcome the young men home. Wives and young women ran to meet them with smiles and kisses, jumping for joy at the sight of them. The children ran around as if they had been shackled for the duration of the men's absence. The older men waved staffs and sticks in the air and beat the ground as if playing the drums. Feasts appeared seemingly from nowhere and music played.

The Druid bard sang songs for their return, telling tales of trophies and riches, green forests, and dark waters. The merry picture lightened the hearts of the weary men, but that did not diminish their satisfaction in revealing the information they had collected while travelling the length and breadth of Brigantium.

It added weight to their homecoming.

The Druid Filid was also present. They sat with the people and listened to the reports. A stag was sacrificed on the Druid table, and the Druids gathered to read the intestines and innards. Dugall was gifted in predictions from such sacrifices, so spread the entrails over the table. A small crowd gathered and waited for and utterance from Dugall, a sign from the gods of good fortune in the coming times. Dugall stood for some time, with his eyes closed. His brow furrowed for but a moment, before his eyes opened wide, up to the sky.

'I see good things for the people here,' he said. The gods have promised victory in battle, and food on your tables, in this coming year.' The people cheered. Then the hung the stag onto the spit for roasting.

That night, there was feasting and drinking, dancing, and coupling with passion. Edric gave thanks to Cerdic and Bryth for saving his life from a watery grave. They were applauded with blessings and good cheer. The young girls danced in front of them, swinging their skirts and hips, suggesting more than a dance. Each young man moved toward the maiden of their choice, swinging them round in a furious swirl.

Bianna, happy to have Edric back, nevertheless, was concerned when she learned of his watery trial. She looked toward Dugall who was sharing huge cuts from the stag among the people.

'Dugall, I am concerned for Edric's health,' she whispered in his ear.

Dugall put the knife down on the serving table and pulled Bianna into the midst of the dancing.

'Tonight, Bianna, you will not worry about Edric. The stag entrails *augur* the gods are with him. There is more. May I speak with you soon?' Not waiting for an answer, Dugall took her hand and in rhythm with the music, swung her round and round.

Edric joined in, choosing one of the village girls who had long been of interest to him. Her name was Ediva. She was seventeen years old and Edric had spent one summer with her three years ago, when he allowed her to join her brother, Teirnan, and the band of lads as they created havoc in the area. They enjoyed battle games that Edric instigated, and Ediva did not shy away from the rough and tumble of the trainee warriors. They spent many sunny days exploring the land beyond the sept, relishing the battle training and wrestling.

Ediva was a strong, pretty girl who joined in as one of the team. She cared very much for Edric, but when Edric and Tiernan argued, it changed everything.

Tiernan had run to her, at the time of the falling out. 'Sister, attend to me,' he bid, holding his ear to stop the blood running down his face and arm. He warned Ediva of his feelings.

'I hate him. He has ridiculed me and made me to be smaller than my own stature.' Spittle ran from the side of his mouth as his anger boiled out of his heart. Ediva reasoned with him, but Teirnan was unforgiving. 'Too many times have I felt the burning of his domineering, but now he has fetched blood. I have had enough. I am leaving,' he vowed. Ediva, clung onto his arm, trying to stop him from leaving. 'It is no good, Ediva. I am going. Come with me. We could start a new life somewhere where I will be accepted, regardless of my measly height.'

But there had been talk in the village about a possible marriage between Ediva and Edric, so Ediva had stayed. 'I will be back, Ediva, and when I do, Edric will be sorry.'

Edric did not want to remember the fight with Tiernan, nor did he want to commit to a wife before he had come of age and seen something of the world.

'But tonight, I will dance with Ediva,' he thought as he took her hand. He searched her eyes for that past spark, but her eyes were not Maawan's. As he danced, he knew that Maawan's body was the only one he wanted to be near; to feel her neck, her lips, and to caress her.

'That which seems so far away, has captured my heart and my need,' he thought. 'I have seen her defiance when facing Taexalin; her strong spirit in the face of danger. She is a woman with soul, and with ability. She had hooked me like a prize fish.'

Ediva, trying to make conversation, asked, 'It must have been hard for you, travelling so wide an area, and in mortal danger from our many enemies, Edric. Would you like to talk about it? I am here for you.' She stroked his hand as she spoke. Edric, drawn back from his disconsolate thoughts, responded, 'How is Tiernan? I haven't seen him for these past two years. Where is he?'

Ediva was vexed at his lack of attention and shrank away from Edric. 'He drew into himself,' she answered. 'I worried about him, but he left one day, saying he was determined to become a warrior. I do not know where he is.' But as she spoke, she looked away. Edric knew she was lying.

As the music changed, Edric bid goodnight to Ediva and left the gathering; a whisp of a shadow hovered nearby. Edric shivered.

Bianna watched as Edric moved toward the Great Hall, and seeing the sadness on his face, wanted to encourage her brother. She chased after him.

'Edric, why are you leaving so soon? Are you ill?' Edric shook his head, but continued on, ignoring Bianna's concerns. 'May I suggest that a good night's sleep is needed? Tomorrow is another day, Edric. Who knows what is ahead?' she coaxed.

Edric silently closed the door, stopping her from entering. 'Good night.' he said.

Dugall came into the hall looking for Bianna.

'What is it, Dugall?' she asked.

'I want to tell you of the omen I have seen tonight, Bianna. While I read the entrails of the sacrificed stag, I had a vision. It was not the time to share it, among the people, but I want to tell you now. I saw the invaders marching to Deva, and then on to Ynys Môn against the shape-shifters and teachers of our faith. I see the time is drawing close when we must be prepared for a journey. The gods will warn us of the time, but we must be prepared.'

Bianna wasn't sure what Dugall required of her, but she poured a cup of mead for the Druid and sat with him. He sat quietly for a moment or two, then looked at Bianna.

'Bianna, I need a wife. Will you honour me with your hand?'

Bianna was taken aback by this proposal. She knew that Dugall had always favoured her, but she did not expect this.

'I will give you an answer in the morning, after I have spoken to my Lord Edric,' she said. Dugall was satisfied. He rose and left the room, his long black mantle falling to his feet. It swirled round his body rustling like falling leaves chanting an incantation.

That night, when Bianna lay in her bed, she thought about all that had happened that day, and of the dreams and visions she had received while Edric was away.

She had seen in her waking dreams, a princess hidden in a Druid fog, all the while men searching for her; some to love her and some to kill her. Bianna had mixed feelings about the visions. She could not decide why she felt hatred one minute yet love another. Nothing made sense to her. And now Dugall had asked for her hand. How did she feel about that? She realised some time ago that she loved him, but never thought of him as a husband. She had accepting her place as prophetess by his side, but marriage was another thing. Nevertheless, a thought nagged at her.

'Maybe this is my destiny,' she pondered. 'Maybe this is what I am meant to be.'

As the thought grasped her mind, a strange peace flowed through her body, as tangible as water flowing over her, should she lie down in a river. It was warm and comforting. She relaxed into the feeling and before a minute had passed, she was sleeping.

By the time morning light broke through the cracks under the roof of her room, Bianna knew she would agree to become Dugall's wife. Talking to Edric was but a courtesy. She rose, dressed, and went to wake her brother. She found him already risen and beginning to dress.

He had been to the stream to wash and looked brighter and livelier than he had on his return from the search. He greeted Bianna as she entered the room. 'Good morning, little sister. Shall we break the fast together?'

The table in the great hall was already filled with good food. Edric took some pears and some bread before turning to Yetta, who was standing ready to serve her lord. 'Can I have some eggs, pork, cakes, and milk?' he ordered, though kindly. Yetta disappeared into the kitchen to arrange the food. Bianna sat by her brother at the table and took some bread. She began to eat it, while waiting for the right moment to give Edric the news.

'Well, Bianna. What has been happening while I have been away?'

'Everything has been well. The older men hunted, bringing in boar, deer, and fish for the table. We have been amply fed. There have been three new babes born in the village, and five young warriors have finished their training in battle. The farmers have had a good harvest. The weather has been kind this year,' she recounted.

'And what of the crown? What of the invaders here and near? What of our murderous, treacherous queen? Have the Romans pilfered more of our land, taking our precious metals; our iron and silver?' Edric asked.

Bianna divulged the news she had received while Edric had been away. 'The queen has travelled north from Isurium, gathering support from her people to war against Venutius,' she explained. 'Two travellers from Parisii brought news from the borders. They told us that Venutius is gathering support to war against the Roman protectorate and is looking for supporters from the Brigantine people who oppose the queen.

Meanwhile, there is rumour that legions are heading toward the Druid colony on Ynys Môn, travelling through Deceangli as we speak.'

'So, there is little time to rest. Civil war is close, and war against the invading army is closer. Edric responded thoughtfully, his face tensing as he spoke. He rose from his seat and began pacing round the room. 'What of the Iceni; our brothers over the border southeast of Parisii? Is King Prasutagus and his wife, Boudicca preparing to join us?' questioned Edric.

'Yes. They are almost ready. Even though Prasutagus allied with the Romans, their interference in Iceni internal affairs has triggered a revolt. They are conspiring with the Trinovantes, and together they plan to bring a revolt against the invaders travelling from the south. Two summers will bring the reward,' Bianna added, 'Queen Boudicca has invoked the goddess Andraste. Her victory is secure.'

Edric nodded. 'Then these days beginning Samheim will be our preparation, too.'

Edric began to eat the food placed before him, with a hearty appetite. Bianna joined in, choosing some of the ham that had arrived on a platter from the kitchen. 'Edric,' she said, hesitantly. 'Dugall has asked for my hand.'

Edric dropped his knife on the table and turned to look at Bianna. 'And have you accepted?' he asked, his expression neutral.

'I believe I will accept, brother, if it pleases you,' she said. Edric's serious face became the broadest grin his sister had ever seen. He jumped up from the table and grabbed her hands, pulling her up and swinging her round.

'Wonderful,' he said. 'Wonderful! My little sister is to take her place with the priesthood. Wonderful!' His excitement at the prospect was contagious, and before Bianna could stop him, he had called through the door for Dugall Dubthach to come.

Dugall entered the hall, with apprehension. He bowed low in front of Edric. Edric could not contain his glee, and grabbed the Druid, hugging him until Dugall wondered for his life. Edric had great respect for the Druid's ability as judge and seer, but also as a warrior. He had fearlessly fought alongside Edric's father, Lord Bloodeworthe, and in the midst of many battles, with raised hands and staff, he had called to the gods to bring victory. This Druid was no ordinary Druid. He was to be feared and revered.

'Brother,' greeted Edric, and reached for the hand of his sister. 'With my blessing, dear brother,' he said, as he passed Bianna's hand to Dugall, who took it and bowed. At that moment as their fingers touched, a wind rushed into the hall fanning open the black Druid cloak and blowing it wide, like two giant wings. His long under garment of white revealed a gold chain round his waist, which jangled a call to the birds outside. In reply, the birds began to call to each other as if singing a spring love song. Through the room the wind blew until there was no telling from which direction it had come. It whirled round Dugall's cloak before leaving as swiftly as it appeared; the cloak settling round Dugall's feet once more.

The morning of the marriage was warm and sunny. Bianna woke with a light heart. Over the past week, she and Dugall had spent much time together, talking and planning, realising that they had been in harmony for many years.

Dugall told his bride how much he had admired her, how he had watched as her seer abilities had grown and how he had begun to love her. 'Do you remember the first time that you stretched out to allow the river to run over you, and you panicked as the water covered your face?' Dugall asked, laughing at the memory.

'And then you lifted me and I saw for the first time, a vision in the clouds above. Yes. I remember. I was frightened, but you showed me how to 'see' much more than I ever knew was there, hidden. You taught me how to move through fear and into a place of peace and magic. Now I know where the doorway lies, and how to pass through,' she whispered, almost as if a spell had been woven, and she did not want to break it.

'And the first time you tried weaving the 'fog.' Do you remember?'

'I forgot the words and got a mist so thick I lost myself,' she laughed.

'But you learned how to spin the mist, and now it is but a simple thing to you,' Dugall encouraged Bianna. She realised that when she was with Dugall, she felt safe and comforted. She felt like a small bird in the hand of a powerful protector. He made her happy.

Dugall whispered in her ear, 'I have stood by your side all these days, watching you grow from a young spirited, giggling girl, into the beautiful woman you are now. I have watched as you grew in the ways of the Druid too, in dignity and sensibility. I have been there since the beginning of your journey, and I want to be by your side at the ending too.' A sweet smell of lavender pervaded the room as they spoke.

Bianna didn't feel hungry enough to break fast that morning. Although she appeared outwardly calm and relaxed, inside her mind was racing. She imagined her mother at her side, giving her warm advice on how to make a husband happy and keep him faithful. She imagined her father holding her and promising a good future with Dugall Dubthach. A tear escaped and trickled down her cheek. How she wished her mother and father could be there to bless her day and hold her hand as she stepped into this new life role. She missed them both.

'Stop this self-indulgence, Bianna. This is your wedding day, not a battle front,' she told herself. With a deep breath, pushing nerves away, Bianna stood erect, as she knew she must, in readiness for her new position to begin.

Bianna had bathed early that morning in the stream, and the women brought fragrant flowers, scents, and oil to anoint the bride's body. Yetta and Osma came into the room giggling and chattering about the great goings-on before them. 'It's a wonderful day, Bianna,' chirped Yetta.

'You need a proper breakfast. The day will be a long one,' suggested Osma, as they carried fruit and wine to the table, and encouraged Bianna to eat at least some of the ripe blackberries and hazel nuts so she would not feel faint during the ceremony. They also brought in a white dress made of linen and a white cloak. 'Oh, Bianna! You will look so wonderful. I wish it was me getting married today.'

Bianna remained quiet. Her head, full of thoughts, gave no room for speech. Her hands trembled a little as she searched in the trinket box that had belonged to her mother. She chose a gold belt and torc. She chose the blue ceremonial bodice too. Her shoes were delicate cream leather, stitched by the Brigantine shoemaker, famed for his dainty work. Each stitch he made with gold thread, embroidered on both shoes the Taranis wheel symbol.

One of the women from the village brought holly, laurel, and berries from the forest near the sept, and wove them into a crown. Bianna looked beautiful as she walked out of the bedroom and into the great hall.

Edric wore the red cloak and a torc of bronze. He stood tall by the side of his sister and kissed her. 'This is a special day: when you become a priestess; but more than that, you become a wife. Father and mother would have been proud this day. And so am I. Little sister, I give you my blessing. Want for nothing. Live your life. Be happy.' He took her hand and led her to the waiting crowd in the circle of houses.

They walked toward the gate and into the forest beyond the sept. The villagers followed. A bower between two great oaks had been raised within a circle of trees. The bower was covered in holly, laurel, and autumn flowers. Buntings of different coloured linens had been woven into the floral bow also.

Dugall waited under the arbour for his bride to appear. He wore a long white Druid's cloak over his white tunic. His chain belt glistened against the white fabric as he walked a little way to watch Bianna approach. He had tied his long dark hair back into a plait, and a golden sash was wrapped round his forehead. His feet had boots of brown, tanned leather; polished till they shone. The smile on his face accentuated his rugged good looks. He was a gentle but impassioned man, and this day it was the gentle side of him which shone the stronger.

The Druids, in their different capes and cloaks, lined the path to the great trees. The bard Druids also wore white, with swan feathers as shoulder capes. They sang songs with great harmonies as the bride approached the circle. Bianna and Dugall faced each other in the centre of the ring. A hush came over the proceedings as Maccar, being charge of the ceremony, began to pronounce the wedding rituals.

He stroked his long beard, as he proceeded to move toward the couple. 'We gather here in peace for this sacred occasion, the marriage between our priestess, our Lady Bianna Bloodeworthe of Gabri-antovices, and Dugall Dubthach the Brown, the High Druid of our people,' he continued. 'As this circle is woven and consecrated, this moment in time and this place becomes blessed. Let us call to the spirits of the four quarters of our world, to our families and our tribe and to our ancestors before us, that this rite be blessed by the powers of all Creation.' The people began to walk slowly round the tree circle sun-wise, led by Maccar, who chanted as he walked. The people responded: 'So let it be.'

'May Peace flow from the East,'
'So let it be.'
'May Peace flow from the South,'
'So let it be.'
'May Peace flow from the West,'
'So let it be.'
'May peace flow from the North,'
'So let it be.'
'May peace, passion, and power
flow through this union,
Today and every day,'
'So let it be.'

As the people came to rest around the outer edges of the tree clearing, Edric moved into the centre of the circle and stood in front of Bianna. The Druid called for quiet, pronouncing:

'Listen to the words of Edric Beornraed, High Breehin; Our Lord Bloodeworthe of Gabrantovices.'

Edric called out loudly to the crowd. 'This day it is my honour and pleasure to hand my sister to Dugall Dubthach, Druid extraordinary, judge and priest to our people.' He turned to Bianna and took her hand. From his cloak, he brought Cynifrida's signet ring. He opened Bianna's palm and pressed the ring tightly into it, folding her fingers around it. 'Our mother, Cynifrida, left this ring for you. She wanted you to have it on this special day. It is a sign of her blessing.'

He looked at the crowd once more. 'This day I give Bianna to Dugall in marriage. So it shall be — now and forever,' he said. He bowed low in front of the couple and walked to the outside of the ring. The Druid performed the ritual of Connected Harmony. Dugall and Bianna's hands were fastened together by coloured braids as a symbol that they were now eternally bound together. Dugall promised to love, protect, and care for Bianna all his days. He took his staff and drew in the ground the four symbols of the Druid understanding, all the while speaking out his promise to his bride.

'As the earth is, my body, I give to you this day.
As the air is, my mind I give to you this day.
As the water is, my soul I give to you this day.
As fire is, my spirit I give to you this day.
All that I have and all that I am
I give to you this day.
This I swear under the sun, the moon, and the stars.'

Bianna and Dugall moved through the throng of happy villagers lining the way round the circle, while one by one the sacred ribbons were untied. Each ribbon was granted as a gift to the person untying, a sign of blessing to the receivers. Bianna smiled and thanked her people as she passed.

'I am blessed this day,' she said. 'I am so grateful for you all. Be blessed also, my friends.'

In response, she heard cries of 'Be happy,' 'You are wonderful,' and 'May you be granted fruitfulness and many children.' Dugall also, smiled and waved.

'My friends, this is an auspicious day. May the gods shower their fruitfulness over you, too.' Singing and dancing, they continued to move toward their homes. Dugall took Bianna in his arms with one smooth movement, spinning her round the grassed expanse in the centre of the sept as the bards started to play their instruments; drums beating a steady rhythm, flutes and whistles made of elder wood blowing out sweet melodies to dance by. For a moment, the people watched, but it was only a short time before the green was packed with folk joining in the dance; swinging each other round in time to the drum beats as they celebrated the marriage union of Bianna and Dugall Dubthach.

The people lit bonfires and began not only to celebrate the newlywed couple, but also Samheim. The feasting and drinking continued through the week, with pigs and cows sacrificed, then roasted and shared from spits built over fires all around the sept. Everyone dressed up in skins and animal heads; families joining with other families shared food and drink. The children played games together and the young men challenged each other in fighting and wrestling, sword play, and axe throwing. The older men sat in groups, reminiscing about battles and women, while the older women read palms and entrails, looking all the while to the future, and young women danced and cavorted with the brightest champions.

At the end of the last day, they gathered round the fires to tell stories of the dead, to celebrate life and to enjoy being part of the whole tribal family of Gabrantovices and Brigantia. The whole village was filled with music and singing, old songs and new, on this New Year's Eve.

Dugall took the hand of his new bride and silently they slipped away.

CHAPTER SEVEN

YULE
Midwinter

G ABRANTOVICES SEEMED TO SLEEP. The weather had turned bitter, and the winds blew across the Northern Sea. Fires burned long and bright in the homes of the people, and from the outside, one could be forgiven for assuming that the occupants would be sitting around their fires, waiting for Imbolc.

In fact, every home was a hive of industry. The fires in the furnaces, usually there to make ironware adornments for cloaks and capes, were being used to forge weapons and spear tips in greater number than ever before. The arsenal was growing. The men were sharpening swords and making new shields, while others whittled at poles to create spear shafts. The women wove woollen clothes and made new blankets, hoods, capes and cloaks, tunics, and leg warmers. Some wove flax into linen, heavier than the usual weave. Some tanned furs, preparing them as outer garments, horse saddles, water sacks, and shoes. Everyone was employed. Even the children collected firewood to keep the fires burning.

There was a continuous, quiet determination to use the time to full advantage. Edric had told them of the need to be prepared, and everyone took it upon themselves to find a way of helping with the preparation. Warriors practiced their skills, while the old men encouraged them in their endeavours. Although Edric had not told them all that he knew, the men understood the seriousness of the position; that not only must they be ready to attack the enemy from Rome, but also to defend their lands and their way of life.

When Yule arrived, it was as if the village almost missed the festival, so preoccupied they were. But just as snow appeared on the hills beyond the sept, someone started to fetch holly and ivy to make decorations for the Yule feast. This spurred another person to ride out to hunt, returning two days later with boar and stag. Before long, the entire village had halted their enterprise to celebrate Yule, even before winter was in full season.

Each week Edric sent out teams of scouts, two or three together. One member of the team was to return with news within the week; and all must return by the next moon phase. Edric did not want his men out for too long through these harsh nights. He needed them to be fit and healthy when the time came for action.

Edric's thoughts drifted to the scout he appointed years ago. He missed Tiernan.

'Teirnan the Tiny,' Edric thought, realising that he hadn't got the best out of Tiernan, and possibly he should have been kinder. But they were young, and he was arrogant. Guilt swelled in his heart as he remembered. 'Tiernan didn't deserved my harsh words, nor my anger. I was haughty,' thought Edric. 'That is no way to encourage the best from people. I should have taken him alongside and reassured him; allowing his confidence to grow."

As he pondered, a large bat flew overhead flapping its cloak-like wings so close that Edric felt the air shift and the creature's damp smell waft to his nose. Edric followed the flight as it settled in a hollow of an oak tree nearby. A ghostly sensation crept upon Edric till the hairs on his neck stood up. 'Am I being watched?' he asked himself.

Edric remained in the sept with a small circle of fighting men and Druids; Dugall included, as first among the wise men and strategists. Wulf-nud was the first to return.

'We scouted to the north and around the east coast of Brigantia, asking after the queen and her Roman allies. We learned that she travelled north, heading toward Vindolanda some months ago, before Samheim. She was escaping Venutius' men, who had routed Eboracum and razed the town. She has sent for Roman support and is holding up somewhere near the Textoverdi. We cannot say more.'

Three weeks later Biticus returned, glad to get home and in from the biting weather. He stood before the council. 'Venutius has travelled home to the Carvetti and is stationed at Luguwalion. He is gathering stronger troops from Loporcares and tribes in that area. They intend to travel toward the southern border at Mamucium, waiting there until other rebel warriors can join them,' he announced. 'Romans are amassing and marching along the Coritani border toward Deva; but they won't venture to battle until after Beltane. Their journey is treacherous, and the foreign soldiers are not used to the hard terrain over the mountains. No guide will help them. We can make sure that they do not use the pass, diverting them across the highest and hardest points.'

Edric nodded. 'Then this is an opportunity to join Venutius and help head off the Roman legions before they reach Deva. If the invader's plan is to attack the rebel Brigante from the southwest, then this makes sense. We can travel down to Boracum, and then on to Mamucium before Beltane and be ready when Venutius arrives there.'

The Druids agreed, so a plan of action was formulated for twenty of the best warriors to head down to the border. At Eboracum, they would divide, with half of the men continuing on the route to meet Venutius, where they would rally against the Roman legion heading north to meet with Cartimandua and her armies. The other half, led by Boreus, one of the older warriors in the sept, were to move directly south from Eboracum toward Vincobancia and from there head to intercept any legion travelling toward Mancunium. Such legions would be diverted toward Odin's shivering mountain pass, through the gorge at Windgates, to be attacked from both sides; or better still, to stop them heading toward Deva, before their arrival at Man Tor.

Edric called for Dugall at the end of the parley. 'Dugall, I am concerned about the queen gathering her armies. I plan to take another troop and travel north. If I can intercept her, ambushing her near Hopocares or even further south toward the border, then I may be able to stop her armies from joining with the legions. Capturing Cartimandua would give us and Venutius a stronger position against the Romans.' Edric was also thinking about how he might deal with the murderer of his father, should he capture her. Although he had been privy to his father's war plans in the past, Edric was new to strategic battle thinking and needed the advice of his judge and seer.

Dugall was quiet for a moment before he responded. 'I will give you an answer in the morning, Edric. It sounds like a good plan, but I would ask for time so I may seek the god's guidance for your success.'

'Till tomorrow then.' Edric nodded, and each went their way.

Dugall left to return to his wife. Bianna smiled when she saw him approaching and began to question Dugall the moment he entered the room.

'Let us sit and eat first, Bianna, and then I will tell you all.'

After their meal, they sat in front of the fire. With linked fingers, Dugall spoke of the plan to join with Venutius against the Romans, and of Edric's request for guidance. Bianna gently probed for more information.

'What of Deva? Is it possible that the Romans intend on using Deva as a camp before taking Ynys Môn? Surely, they would not dare.'

'Indeed, they would, Bianna. The Romans make no secret of their hatred of our practices. We hold much power over our people; a power that Claudius believes belongs to him.' They sat in silence for a while each chasing their own thoughts, watching the embers in the pit. The fire crackled as a brown Druid added logs and charcoal and once again the flames rose high. The heat from the flames warmed their hands as they interlocked, until it felt to each of them that they were as wax, melting into each other. The wax ran toward the fire, embracing the blaze, until they were alight and part of the red and gold coals. Each of their bodies shaped into a bird rising from the flames, and once again, Bianna took to the heavens, flying high and over her land. Dugall followed, with no less strength.

They flew out of the sept and over the moors. Looking down, they could see the water surrounding Ellestob glistening in the sunlight. Beyond that, Maawan was riding on a pony with a warrior protector by her side. The birds flew over the travellers, listening to their conversations. They were headed north toward Vindolanda, and toward the queen. The two raptors kept watch, picking up sounds and movement around the travelling duo. Above the travellers, a dark cloak-like cloud had gathered. Suddenly, from the centre of the blackness, lightning exploded as daggers, cutting and stabbing. A shaft of light shot through the air toward Maawan, gathering momentum as it rolled round and round. Maawan looked up. Just above her head was a spear of fire. She would not be able to avoid it. Everything seemed to be happening in slow-motion. Dugall appeared at her shoulder, reaching for the thunder-strike as it bolted, catching the end of it in his talons. The lightning hit the bird, shooting a staff of pure light though his body. Bianna, with impossible speed, grabbed hold of Dugall. She darted away from Maawan before the spear could reach its target, carrying Dugall to safety.

By the time Bianna and Dugall returned from their visions, the fire had died low. The room was full of shapes and shadows. Bianna was the first to wake, with a heavy head. The dream was portentous, and the darkened room made it linger in her mind. Dugall took longer in rousing from his 'sleep.' He rubbed his burned hands and tried to stand but could not.

Bianna held him for a while, caressing his hands again, opening them to inspect the charred skin on the palms. She fetched clean coverings for the wounds, patting a mixture of salt and water onto them then tying the covering over them.

They did not speak all the while. Bianna helped Dugall to bed, staying by his side. Exhausted, and sore, the two fell asleep in each other's arms.

Before morning light, Bianna, fully awake, went to the shrine by the doorway of Dugall's grove, bringing water and bread as an offering for the table. She knelt, seeking clarity for the visions of the night before. As her mind settled, she was startled by a rustling in the trees beyond the grove. She got up to investigate. A stag was trapped in the thicket. She went to help the animal escape, untying his legs from the brambles, but stopped when she heard voices. She crept toward the source of the sound, listening in to the conversation. Two men were discussing the plans which had just been made: for the journey to join Venutius and Edric's planned raids. One was a voice she thought she recognised, but where she had heard it eluded her. The other voice was new to her.

'I will send word when they have left the sept. You will be able to intercept them en-route,' the familiar voice ordered.

'My men will be ready. Cartimandua will pay well for their heads.'

'Do not forget, you owe me half the trophies and gold collected. And I want my share of the head coins too.'

There was a gruff grunt, as the other replied. 'Hmm. You'll get your share when the deed is done, and I have received rewards from our queen.'

Bianna tried to peer through the thicket to see which two traitors were willing to betray their lord to Cartimandua. She stepped forward, but a twig by her shoulder snapped, warning the subversives of their dangerous situation. Halting, they signalled to each other to search in the direction of the sound. Bianna stood her ground, raised her arms, and began to circle slowly. In a whisper, she recited in the old tongue; nervously hoping that the incantation would perform:

'Ceo draoidheachte,
Cover her head,
Cover her feet,
Over Bian,
Ceo draoidheachte.'

A boggy mist rose from the ground, thick and white, as quickly as the turning of the deer. The men stumbled in the thick mist, confused as to where the fog had come from so suddenly. The air was heavy. Covering their mouths, they tried not to cough, but found that the vapours made them gag. Bianna saw one of the men run into the opening just beyond the shrine. She saw his green woven cloak, his *bracae* and a tunic made of red and green woven wool. She knew she would remember him again. She looked for the other man; the one whose voice she recognised. He was nowhere to be seen. Above Bianna, hovering like a Druid cloak, was the dark cloud she had seen in her vision the night before. Filled with a terrible sense of foreboding, Bianna began to quake. She stood in the midst of the Druid fog and watched until the cloud disappeared. Frozen to the spot she did not dare move. She lowered her arms slowly, and the fog sank to the ground.

Checking around her, Bianna took a tentative step. She stood again for a moment, listening, while every hair on her body stood on high alert. Again, she glanced slowly around, making sure that she was safe to move. She saw a small white flower at her feet. She picked the winter rose, taking it with her as she returned to the grove.

Dugall was up and waiting for her return. 'Where have you been?' he asked with concern.

Bianna began to tremble. Dread rose in her chest as she explained what she had overheard. Her heart raced; she was breathless as she went over the event.

'Then we must warn Edric immediately. If there is a traitor in the camp, we need to find out who it is,' Dugall said.

'Wait,' called Bianna, for Dugall was already marching toward the door. 'Dugall, there is more.' She told him of the Druid fog, and the way she had conjured the mist to make herself invisible. 'There was a blackness above and although I was hidden in the mist, unseen I am sure from the ground, I'm not sure that the shadow above me was so blinded.'

'What of the shadow, Bianna?' asked Dugall. 'Everything in me tells me it is a curse; a watcher has hooked onto us. We must be very careful. Someone with these sorts of skills is holding much power.'

'Was there not a similar dark cloud overhead in the vision last night? I agree. it could be a Druid with shape shifting powers, but who? How many of our sort are accomplished in such ability? What of the vision last night? What of the dark cloud chasing Maawan? What does it all mean, Dugall?'

At this, Dugall became agitated. When he spoke, it was with conviction.

'Bianna, yesterday's vision is a warning: an order from the gods. Maawan must be very important to their plans. Are we being called to watch over her and protect her?' he asked, more to himself than to Bianna.

Bianna went to his side. 'But for now, you must separate your thinking away from the fight you had planned, I think,' suggested Bianna. 'We should be embarking on another path, at least for the next few months. It might become clearer as we travel this path. Did you not tell me that we should prepare for a journey? You said, 'The time is coming when the gods call to the four winds, the Fire, and the High One will return.' Is this not such a time, Dugall, my love? We must ready quickly, for this is our fate.'

Bianna reached for his hand, as she so often did. She wanted to soothe him and calm his thinking. She wanted to caress the man she had married, this strong warrior priest. The passion flowed through her fingers like sparks that fly from the sun; hot and dangerous. Dugall jumped as the power surged through his hand, and up his arm. He fell to the floor shaking.

Both knew that this was a sign pointing to the purpose of their union. Both understood that the purpose was significant.

The following morning the winter rain fell heavily on the ground, creating deep puddles in the sept. The priest and priestess made their way to Edric, avoiding the water underfoot as best they could. The wide hoods on the brown cloaks they had chosen were pulled down, hiding their faces. They approached Edric, signalling with fingers to their lips, that they wanted to speak in private. Edric got up from the bench by the fire in the hall and made his way to the bedroom. Bianna and Dugall followed as shadows.

Once inside Edric's room, away from any eavesdroppers, they explained the vision they had shared.

'We must find Maawan, Edric. She is in danger,' Bianna explained. 'We don't understand why, but it's important that we do. The gods have dictated our obedience.' Bianna did not share her assumption of who Maawan might be. Bigger things were at stake. Edric was keen to find Maawan too, so he had no problem with their decision.

'But, what about advancing on Cartimandua? Am I still to journey north?' he asked.

Dugall had already anticipated Edric's question. 'Yes, Edric. We all go north together. We have seen where Maawan is travelling, and we will make our way there. Then we will hold Maawan until further visions reveal the god's plan for her. You may go on from there, to capture Cartimandua, as you see fit.'

Bianna took her brother's hand, looking him straight in the eye and began to tell him of the treachery she had overheard. 'I would recognise him again, but I cannot recall where I heard the voice before.' She looked away, trying to recall the voice. 'In a vision, perhaps? Or maybe closer to home…'

Edric sat in the chair by the bedroom fire, despite the intense heat, he shivered.

'That is why our journey plans must not be shared with anyone. Even the company of men chosen to travel with us must not know where, or why we travel,' Bianna continued. She stalked about the room, shaking her head. 'I wish I could recall where I have heard that voice. He sounded so very familiar…'

They talked for another hour or so, making plans for the *ambaxtoi* and deciding who they could trust to take the journey with them. Three men were chosen to accompany them: Buite, Beored, and Wulfnud. They discussed who would take charge of the sept while they were away, deciding to leave the security of the people in the hands of the Druid Maccar, seer and priest with authority. It was agreed that Dugall would give the word when the time came to leave: the gods would reveal it.

Walking a short way from the sept toward the Northern Sea, overlooking the bay, Bianna planted the white rose she had picked in the woodlands. As she planted, she prophesied.

'This day I plant the Rose of Brigantia, the flower of Albion. I plant so that the seeds from this flower may flourish and grow, even as the spirit of Brigantia may flourish. And Albion also.'

CHAPTER EIGHT

DYN HYSBYS
Wizard

WINTER WRAPPED ICY fingers round the mountain paths from Ellestob to Epiakon. Snow lay heavy on the ground; fog spread wide across the stony crags, making it almost impossible to travel the drover's road. Only wild sheep dared to venture across the hard land, looking for grazing and shelter.

Camulo led Maawan onwards toward Cauldron Snout, with the intention of finding a camp for the night. The snow was turning into a blizzard. Maawan wrapped the cloaks and furs around her face and body, but the cold wind gouged her hands until she could not feel them. Still, the horse and pony continued, heads bent against the harsh frozen rain.

The path north had led them east across moorlands and towards the mountain range known as The Peneinz. From this direction, they approached the mountains which were divided north and south by a valley with a river running the length of it and back toward the Northern Sea. They journeyed up the river, coming across a waterfall, with a cave beneath. It was here that they dismounted, making their way into the cave across steppingstones and high ridges. The cave was big enough to house the horse and pony, and although it was damp from the waterfall beyond, it was safe. The weather showed no sign of calming that day, so Maawan was pleased to stay in the cave until her fingers had thawed.

She looked round the cave. At the back, it was less damp. There were signs of other visitors having used this shelter: a fire pit had been hollowed out of the hard ground, and a small stack of wood had been left high on a stone ridge. There was also a flint stick, so before the horses were unsaddled, Camulo had begun to build a small fire.

That night, with the sound of water loud enough to make conversation impossible, they sat warming themselves while the outer cloaks and skins dried. They ate some of the food prepared before they left Ellestob, aware that they may need to limit the amount they used, should the journey take longer than they had planned. Both slept.

The morning light brought little change, so for most of the day they stayed inside the cave. On the third day, Camulo rose early, venturing outside to collect whatever wood he could find from the small copse near the river. He brought back a cape full of sticks and twigs. Every hour he went again, seeking and collecting whatever he could find to keep them warm. Maawan exchanged his wet cloak for a dryer one, spreading the blankets and cloaks out along the rocks, allowing them to dry as quickly as possible. She was grateful for the abundance of water to drink, but Maawan would have liked the noise to be less deafening.

It was a week before the snow eased and the sun dwindled weakly through the cloud; it was enough of an omen to bring hope to the travellers. They packed the horses again and wrapped themselves in the dried clothing. Leading the horses carefully out of the cave and over the riverbed, they continued their journey northwest, following the river.

Knowing they would again need to find better shelter from the worst of the weather, they headed upwards, passing Cauldron Snout, hoping to find a safe place. The cascading water ran over steps and ridges like a giant causeway, and into the large bubbling cooking pot below. They made slow progress; climbing higher by the snow-covered banks of the carousing river, overshadowed by massive whin sill cliffs. The two riders continued to follow the waterway, but the mountainous path was arduous. They had been climbing continuously for some hours when the terrain changed and began to fall. From a vantage point they could see the way of their descent. Beyond that, was a juniper wood. It was there that would make camp.

Although the ground was icy hard, the woods made a good shelter from the cold. That night, they hung their cloaks through the branches and knurled curling trunks of the juniper trees, creating a wind shield. Camulo lit a fire and for the first time in many days, they talked.

Maawan shared the last cake she had. It was stale and mouldy, but she picked out the side which was less blue. The salted fish, grilled on the fire, was good and her hunger was abated.

'Have we far to go, Camulo?' asked Maawan.

'I fear for the next leg of our journey, little one. Epiakon is a farmstead owned by Lord Epicus, a friend of mine. He will give us room and food. Epiakon should be a fair place to rest for a while, and we will be able to replenish our food supply,' he replied. 'But the journey will be a tough one, as winter holds power.'

'I have a request, Camulo. Please do not laugh at me. I know I am only a servant girl, but would you teach me to fight like you?'

Camulo could not help himself, and laugh he did, though not unkindly. 'Ha-ha! Little one, why have you need to learn the art?' he questioned.

'I have a dream. I wish to be like you and,' she hesitated, 'and like…Eachann. Not to kill,' she protested, 'but to be able to defend myself should I need to.'

An image of Venutius appeared in her mind.

'Then we will start tomorrow, little one. If you desire to become a warrior, then I will help you,' he promised. That night they slept wrapped together, taking warmth from each other. It seemed to Maawan, that Camulo was like the father she had never known, though she understood that for the first three years of her life, he had taken that place.

She felt secure and safe in his arms.

The morning did not bring better weather. A mist had settled all around, making it hard to see more than a few feet ahead. Gathering their things and packing the horse and pony was not an easy task in the damp dawn of the Pennine Fell. But without breaking fast, they were up in the saddles and on their way. Maawan talked to Camulo, asking him questions about warfare and defence, arms, and battles. Camulo was happy to give information and promised to teach some shielding and resistance moves in case Maawan should ever be attacked.

They ventured through the mist, not really knowing whether the path was underfoot or in another direction, but Camulo was sure that if the land continued to rise, they wouldn't be far from the desired track. Eventually the mist started to clear, and through the veil a short distance in front of them, they could see what appeared to be a small broch, erected from the stone littering the landscape. It was a small structure; a shelter for one, rather than a home. At the side of the doorway to the left, a horse was tethered. Camulo advanced with caution, but just as he was about to dismount to investigate, a young man wearing the speckled cape of a druid in training appeared. He was short and squat, with a torch in his hand; a rod-like piece of wood with a rag wrapped around one end. The animal fat tied to the rag burned brightly, leading the way through the mist to the Druid. 'Hail, my lord and lady. How do you fare?'

'Hail,' responded Camulo. 'We are junketeers from Cauldron Snout, but we seem to have lost our path to Epiakon. We have been travelling through the snow for some days and would value a good rest, warmth, and some food, if you have any. We will pay in coin, or otherwise, kind sage.'

'Come, come,' beckoned the solitary young man. He led them past a bench by the door, which had a gifting bowl atop. A bell hung outside and a small iron shrine with a statuette of a horned god stood also on the bench. The bowl was empty. By the side of the hut, and behind the tethered horse, a sheep pen had been attached, but it was occupied by only a goat. The goat bleated as they passed.

Guiding them into his home the Druid went to the fire where a pot of stew hung. He began to stir the stew. The smell from the pot was strong, but the stench from the fire overpowered the whole room. A sheep carcase had been cut into pieces to burn as fuel. The heat it produced was almost like a furnace, but it allowed both Maawan and Camulo's bodies to begin to thaw. Around the room, supplies of food were stacked against the walls. Sacks of barley and rye rested against one another; dried fish and meat hanging above. A full water pail was positioned on a stool just inside the doorway. A bench and a table big enough for two also rested against the wall. To the other side of the room, a roll of blankets was ready to be laid out on the floor to create a bed for the sage.

Camulo queried, 'Are you alone, sage?'

'Yes, indeed. I am but ten years into my apprenticeship, on my journey to gain knowledge and skill in the art of our religion. I am contemplating the heavens, and their position on earth. The stars show their pathway much clearer on this hill, and I am able to reach out to the gods from here. This is a thin place, where the heavens meet the earth, where doorways are opened to those who would see and those who would dare walk through the fissure,' he explained. Continuing, he spoke in a whisper, 'I seek wisdom from watching the clouds and the flight of birds. I take time to sit and contemplate the sky above. I focus on the stars, asking a question. An answer may streak across my vision or appear symbolically in the clouds. I become one with the world, and the world within me.' For a moment, the young man became almost trancelike, but suddenly remembering he had visitors, snapped out of it, and regained his thoughts. He gestured to the bench.

'Please, sit. I will bring food.'

In silence they waited for bowls to be brought to them. The bowls were filled with some of the stew from the pot, and in due course, Maawan and Camulo were filled.

'My lord, what is your name and the name of your companion?' the Druid asked.

'I am Camulo of Ellestob and this is Milburga.' Camulo hesitated. 'Milburga is my daughter.' Camulo added to deflect any possibility of questioning. We are travelling to find her mistress; we lost her on the journey. She is travelling with two others. Have you seen anything of them, my friend?'

'No one has passed this way since Samheim.'

'Then we must continue our search when we are recovered.'

'Stop this night, my lord,' suggested the Druid.

Camulo nodded gratefully, though he had no idea how three people would find room to spread in such a small space. 'We will indeed, if it is acceptable to you. But first we must know your name.'

'I am vowed to quietness and contemplation, as I seek to know and reveal the unknown. The name given to me is Dyn Hysbys, though I am still learning the ways of Druid magic,' he said. 'I have yet to master any real magic, though I have some small skill in the art of divination.' The Druid, Dyn, began to tell a tale of legend and wizardry, sitting on one of the food sacks. The conversation was light, and it seemed to Maawan, that Dyn Hysbys was practicing his tales, should he ever be allowed into the full Druid grove.

Having seen in the Druids serving her mother, the periods of time required for the development of skills, Maawan knew that up to twenty years of learning was likely before the full art could be embraced. The High Druid of Brigantia, Donn Donnlugh, had been serving for many years before he learned how to weave the spirits and see the future in the sacrificial entrails of animals and humans. She knew only too well of his dark side also; in the way he had looked at her when they were left alone. Maawan did not like the High Druid and shuddered as she was reminded of him.

When it came to sleeping, Maawan once again sought the safety and comfort of her mighty protector. They slept near the fire, wrapped in their own blankets, but tightly packed together, Maawan cuddling up to Camulo as if her life depended on it. Camulo kept one eye on the Druid and one eye on the screen of wattle and moss which covered the doorway.

The mist didn't lift the following day, which made Camulo nervous about venturing beyond the broch, but he felt that the journey shouldn't be delayed any further. Believing that Epiakon was within a day's distance, they packed the horse and pony with intentions of starting off again. But the mist thickened so that it was impossible to see an arm's length away. They abandoned the plan and settled down for another day and night with Dyn. Dyn provided a bowl of rye porridge and some milk. They talked little but watched with interest the workings of the Druid's Day.

He visited the shrine in the early morning, making the daily patterns of prayers to the gods, afterwards feeding his horse and goat. He shared some fodder with Camulo's horse and the pony. All the while Dyn talked to himself. In the old language, he called to the four corners, drawing a circle in the air, seeking through the three rites of 'separation, transformation and return' that he might soon be allowed home. He was lonely and had almost forgotten how to communicate with others. Maawan saw this and wondered.

'Dyn, how long have you been living in this place?' she asked.

'As long as the day is, and six years.'

'Then isn't it time to go back to your town?' she asked, kindly.

'I cannot return until I have passed the test of re-doing. I must sing a song about my transforming, but I can't think of anything. My mind is blocked. Until I can express my changing, I cannot return,' he explained.

'Then we will help you, Dyn. By the fire tonight we will sing, until you have a song in your heart, which you can take back to your home,' Maawan smiled.

That night, when the fire was at its highest, Camulo started to sing an old warrior song, which had been sung by many past warriors, many times. He knew the song by heart, as all Brigante people did. He thumped out a beat with his hand on the table and blasted out the song.

'All through the battle and into the night,
Warriors fighting with all their might.
The fighting men battling with iron and gold,
counting the spoils and glories all told.
We are the victors.
Conquerors bold.
Never will we be the slave.'

Maawan joined in the anthem, enjoying the light-hearted beat. She felt like dancing. If there had been space in the little broch, she would have allowed her feet to catch the beat. Instead, she tapped with her toe, and clapped. It was a while before Dyn learned the words of the song and joined in the chorus.

'We are the victors! Conquerors bold,' he sang. His voice was rusty and off key, but the words came out loud and clear. 'Never will we be slaves!' he shouted.

Taking a breath at the end of many lusty minutes, Dyn got up and went to a space behind the sacks of rye. It had been hidden from sight, but now he revealed a cask, jug, and tankards. Pouring the mead into the tankards, he shared the secreted nectar. They drank, and once more the singing continued. Maawan was next to sing. She sang a love song, made from her heart at that moment, about a warrior saving her from a dark shadow. She sang, allowing the words to flow from her mind, without thought. She sang with a passion that surprised even her, about the warrior being handsome, brave, and fearless. She sang about the death of this brave one as he battled against the shadow. Sadness filled her exquisite voice. The room became quiet, as the three of them felt the emotion of her words. Several minutes passed as if a dream had woven a hiatus between this world and another.

Dyn began to sing:

> *'This world is whirling round and round and life is but a dream.*
> *The stars and heavens open up to life. Not what it seems.*
> *But bigger understanding and brighter falling star,*
> *Bring home the truth, reality, of who we really are.*
> *Earth and Heaven intertwine*
> *Each and every one.*
> *Gold and silver deeply mined; blazing like the sun.'*

The ghostly sounds coming out of Dyn's mouth as he sang the heartfelt song caused the hairs on the back of Camulo's neck to stand up. Maawan stood, and grabbing hold of Dyn's hands, she pressed them together with love.

'Dyn. This is your song! This is your song!' she said softly, but with excitement. Dyn started to weep. That night they slept well.

The following morning, they all packed for the journey. Dyn was excited to travel with them, and they were pleased for him to join them. After all, he knew the way through the still lingering fog, and onwards toward Epiakon. The roughness of the track from the broch to Epiakon was such that for a good stretch of the way, they had to dismount and walk.

There was need to watch every step. But their spirits were high, and the path was not so torturous, should the rain set in.

CHAPTER NINE

ANAM CARA

Soulmate

THE THREE ARRIVED at Epiakon before the gates were shut for the night, in time to find lodgings before the great Druid cloak of darkness descended on the *tunskipe*.

Camulo made haste to talk to his old friend and gather information about the Romans and Cartimandua.

'The Romans were looking to build a fort at Vindolanda and had sent troops to inspect the land and ready it for building,' explained Epicus. 'But many of the soldiers have become quite weary of fighting and travelling. They've settled down with our people living, round about. Some have married our girls, and some of them are here, working on my lands. They help with the ponies, and in exchange, they get a share of them. They will take them to work on the local ore fields. I'm happy to trade with them,' he continued, dismissing the politics of his trading. Epicus had learned quickly that working alongside the Romans was a good way to save his head from being separated from his shoulders, and, although he was a fighting man, he was short in stature, and his family was large. He was a merry man and happy to play a beer trading game with the Romans instead of fighting. Camulo enquired after Cartimandua and discovered that she had been in the area for a few weeks, recruiting soldiers, horses, and northern Brigante to help her in the battle against her rebelling tribes; though Epicus was unable to tell them exactly where the queen was. This information was good, and Maawan expected that she would be able to see her mother in a few moons turns.

"How do the Romans treat your people, Epicus,' enquired Camulo.

'Well enough, so long as they do not try and follow the old ways. The Romans aren't keen to let the Druids have a say in what's going on here, but nothing is actually confronted. It's all behind the wind. They—the Romans—have started erecting shrines to their gods, and encouraging us to worship those, instead of our own. It's subtle, but there is a feeling among the people that we are being deceived, and the queen is being tricked,' he explained.

Maawan was taken aback by this information. 'How can that be, Epicus? The queen has made a pact with the Romans. She retains her lands and power. How can that be undermined?'

'Indeed,' answered Epicus. 'The pact is there for the benefit of the Latins, and the Latins only. As long as Carti defends the Pict and northern tribes from Brigante northern borders, the Romans benefit. Their troops can be deployed in the south, fighting uprisings there. They are happy to let her be. But the changes they bring under the banner of 'ally' are insidious. It won't be obvious until it is too late. We have heard many rumours of torture and starvation perpetrated among southern tribes of Albion as the infiltrators take land and power. There is no such promise of peace there.'

'These are dangerous times, Epicus,' Camulo concurred. Turning to Maawan, he smiled. 'Milburga, do not trouble yourself. Let us complete our quest, then these things can be discussed further.'

Epicus was happy to give the band of travellers' lodgings by the side of the Druid grove, where they settled down to rest until morning. That night, as they ate together, Maawan asked Camulo if he would begin her 'training' in warfare

'When the sun gets up, we will also,' said Camulo. 'There is a place outside the gates where we can meet with privacy and practice the art of self-defence,' he promised her.

Before the cock crowed, Maawan was up, washed and dressed, kneeling by Camulo's side.

'Wake up, Camulo. There is something very special about today, and I am eager to start my lesson,' she begged. Dyn also woke and readied himself.

The three set out to the moorland just beyond Epiakon, to a place high on the moors. The moors were wet and boggy, making the climb arduous, but as they climbed high enough to see the commanding view overlooking the land beyond, they realised the ascent was in every way worth the travail. They stood taking in the vista, breathing the sharp air, before Maawan noticed the stones.

'Dyn, let us make a circle here,' she said. 'We can make an arena for my battle training, but first we can make a shrine to our gods,' she suggested as she held a straight arm, pointing and circling the area she wanted to enshrine.

They worked for the best part of the day, carrying, and placing stones to form a circle. When the work was done, they sat in the circle and rested.

Edric and the others travelled at speed directly from Gabrantovices via the sea road. Heading northwards, they visited a few places on the way, but only as the need for fresh supplies and rest dictated. Within three days they shifted direction westward from the mouth of the Tyne, toward Vindolanda. Little progress was made in the next three days though, as Roman soldiers were dispersed along their route. Edric, wanting to travel without being recognised, realised that they needed to make a detour from the main pathway.

At Corebricg, where the river divides and the tributary ran southwest, the group headed on.

They rested at Linnel, a small farmstead on the banks of what is known as 'The Wicked Waters,' a tumultuous and restless stretch of fast flowing river. A shrine stood on the banks of the gushing torrent. They made camp there, near enough to find shelter among the trees and plants growing up at the side of the river, but far enough away to be safe from the turbulent current. Once they had assembled the bivouac, eaten, and rested, Edric spoke to Buite and Wulfnud.

'I need to know about the queen and where she is stationed. Ride to Vindolanda and bring word of her camp. Make sure you are not seen. I need as much information as you can gather overnight,' he ordered. They set off immediately.

There was a rustling in the trees behind the rough tents. Drawing his sword, Edric signalled urgently to Dugall to cover Bianna. Beored also drew his sword and advanced stealthily into the wood. Edric walked the other way to encircle the area where the noise had come from.

Before they had crept more than two arms lengths, a head popped up from behind a bush and said, 'Thank the gods I have found you.'

The two warriors grabbed the man and dragged him out of the thicket. Beored went to take him from behind and laid his sword over the throat of the interloper.

'Stop! Please, I am from Gabrantovices. I am your own Druid, Lurnan,' he begged.

By this time, Edric and Dugall had joined them. They recognised the brown Druid.

'What are you doing here?' Edric asked.

'I followed you, lord. I thought I might be able to help you. I am a good cook, and I am able to serve you on your travels.' Lurnan explained.

'Did I give you leave to follow, Lurnan? *Burraidh!*'

'No-no lord. I took it upon myself,' he answered. 'I beg your forgiveness. I wanted to help.'

'Then get the food ready tonight, and do NOT speak!' Edric ordered. Edric was anxious that the Druid may have discovered their plans and spoken to others, but for the time being he was relieved that the Druid was one of their own. Turning to Dugall, he said, 'He's one of your lot, Dugall. Take very good care to watch him.'

'My lord,' Dugall assented.

That night, they sat round the fire eating salted fish with bread. Lurnan sat outside the ring, with orders to watch the horses and to be on guard for any more travellers who might pass that way. As they ate, Edric asked Bianna a question that had bothered him for some time.

'Bianna, when I brought Maawan home, before I had time to tell you about her, you said you knew who she was.' He looked her in the eye and continued. 'What did you mean?'

Bianna said nothing for a while but watched the flickering flames of the fire as it danced and sparked. She answered as if in an almost trance-like state.

'That evening, before mother died, and before you returned to make your peace, I had a vision: the crown of Brigantia fallen; the pieces of the kingdom undone, followed by the vision of a red-haired queen wearing a crown of stars, riding on a white horse. I saw the ending and the beginning of a new Brigantia, yes, even a new Albion.'

Edric knew that this vision was profound, but unlike his sister, he was not able to see further than the shoes on his feet. 'Explain, Sister. Please,' he begged softly.

But the trance was broken, and Bianna could not.

She sat in silence for a while longer, staring at the flames, wanting to bask in the memory of the vision. Then, in the fire, she saw again the tumbling crown while she lay outside her house recovering from the smoke, and Yetta fussing over her.

She remembered, in the vision, she had seen someone with a trinket box of powerful portents. She remembered his face, then his voice. She remembered. Slowly she rose. She walked to the outer circle and stood before Lurnan.

'Traitor.' she said, pointing to Lurnan, who was getting to his feet.

His hand was to his sword in a flash, but just as quickly, Beored was up, sword drawn also. Dugall wove a binding spell. Before Edric could rise from his place, the Druid fell as the brambles and tall weeds wrapped themselves round his feet causing him to tumble headlong into the bramble bush. Dashing forward, Dugall grabbed the cloak of the brown Druid and held him. Edric and Dugall tied him to a tree, making sure he was unable to escape. Bianna stood before the traitor.

'You hid in my house! I saw you. You lit rush reeds to make the candle smoke. The house might have gone up in flames, had it not been for Yetta. Your plan didn't work out, did it, Lurnan? Did it?' she questioned. 'You met the other traitor in the woods by the shrine. You planned to give my brother's head for a price. You make me sick,' she said, spitting in the Druid's face.

'Who did you conspire with, Lurnan?' asked Edric, but there was no reply.

'Did you think that by siding with the queen, against your own people, that you would be given a position in the new halls of Claudius?' Bianna laughed at the thought of this and spat again. 'You have given your own people a death sentence.' She turned her back on him at that point, ready to ask for his head, but Lurnan spoke softly to her.

'Do you think you can save Brigantia or Albion, with your spells and weak powers? It is a war that cannot be won by you. It is already too late for that. You are the one killing your people, by not ceding to the emperor Claudius and his new religion.'

Bianna spun round and slapped the Druid across his face with such strength that red welts in the shape of her hand displayed the force of the delivery.

That night, when silence had fallen into sleep, Edric got up and dragged Lurnan into the woods. There, he gave the Druid's head to Belissima, the water goddess, and watched as it was washed away in the strong current.

'One of our own,' whispered Edric. The corners of his mouth quivered as he knelt by the side of the river and asked for forgiveness from the one god he had heard would forgive.

The morning had a crisp, spring-like quality, the air cold but fresh. Dew lay as spangles across the land, giving off a beauty glimpsed for only a moment before disappearing into the reality of the day. Buite and Wulfnud returned in time for breakfast. No one asked after Lurnan. Each knew his end was inevitable.

'News, my men?' Edric slapped the men on the back as they ate the pork left over from the night before. Beored had made rye porridge, and they emptied their bowls quickly.

'The queen is not at Vindolanda. She has already left, and it is suspected that she is going back to Isurium to salvage what she can. She has been promised an auxiliary of Roman soldiers to support her war against Venutius. She is hoping that they will arrive in time for her to take back the lands she has lost,' reported Wulfnud.

Buite added, 'She won't travel far in this weather. I suspect she is just getting out of the area to a safe place to hold up until Imbolc. That's when we will find out where she is.'

The party mounted their horses and set off as directed by Bianna and Dugall, toward Epiakon.

Maawan, Camulo, and Dyn sat inside the circle; watching the sun set the sky ablaze as it began to set. The fingers of red, yellow, and gold spread over the horizon like a fan setting the land in front of them aflame. Maawan sensed a thin veil between her world and the Otherworld; a doorway was being revealed.

Dyn started to sing. It was as if having found his voice, he wanted to sing all the time. He sang a haunting melody, calling the earth to flourish and the heavens to give meaning to the soul. Maawan stood, and feeling at one with the earth beneath her, she also started to sing softly, echoing the melodies flowing from Dyn. She sang in the old language uttering words taught long ago. She sang a tune from the beginning of time; a song calling forth from the darkness of the earth's womb the egregore of light.

Dyn and Camulo moved outside the circle to give her space to call to the earth. She began to dance, moving with the rhythm she alone could hear.

The two men stood in awe and watched as she swayed sunwise around the circle. One step, another, a jump, and another step. Her body moved like long reeds swaying in the wind, forming a slow, hypnotic dance.

As Edric and his band arrived at Epiakon, the sun was already going down. A breeze flowed down from the surrounding moorland. Edric stopped. Listened. Ethereal sounds riding the breeze, brought waves of delicate tunes to his ear. He looked round.

'Have they heard it?' he asked himself. 'Can you hear that?' he asked. Picking up a speed, he rode toward the source of the music. Not too far in the distance, he saw it. Saw her.

Silently Edric advanced toward the source of the music. He stopped, staggered at the image he saw in front of him. A silhouette like no other, as Maawan danced before the fiery sky; bewitching, intoxicating. He sat straight on his horse, not daring to breathe; not wanting to break the spell of the image before him.

Bianna, Dugall, and the others softly dismounted as they approached, and stood in a semi-circle round the stones, near Camulo and Dyn. Silently they watched. Camulo, aware of the approaching intruders, had readied his sword, but the entrancing of the moment held Camulo. He was immovable; detained by the gods.

Slowly, Edric dismounted, and entered the circle. His hand reached out to touch Maawan. She moved round without fear and looked into his eyes. She had felt his presence before he had arrived at the stones. She knew he was coming. He took her hand and pulled her to him.

Dyn, mesmerised by the unearthly scene in front of him, started to sing again. The powerful melody drifted with intensity across the moor, till the blazing sky met the zephyr in response.

Edric and Maawan danced together in front of the setting sun. Their bodies did not need to hear the music, for they were making their own soul sounds. They swayed together. They held one another as they moved in unison; each movement bringing them closer together. He touched her neck, then her shoulder, running a finger down her arm, pulling her to him. He wrapped his arms round her body, moving with tenderness as they swayed into each other.

The fire was awakening.

As they twisted and twirled Maawan's golden red hair fell loose over her shoulders. Suddenly, it was swept up by a gust of warm breeze, until her hair became part of the fiery clouds above. She reached high and Edric reached too. Their arms became an interlinked coil, embracing the heavens. A firestorm spat from their fingertips, fused together as a golden spiral. Fire bolts shot into the sky, until Maawan and Edric could not be distinguished from the sky, the earth, or from each other.

A flock of golden *plover* rose in unison from the moors, rising high above the circle; swooping, and singing the chorus of Dyn's song. They flew round the circle three times, before the black cloak appeared, menacing and impenetrable; the darkness fell. It spread across the horizon, to the edges of the ring, flaying out wide to cover the moor.

In the billowing shadow, the birds were captured. Dugall, sensed danger. '…Great peril here for these two,' he thought. Urgently shapeshifting, he rose as one of the birds, eclipsing the darkness, wrenching it to the ground. He; the one bird to escape, fell with the darkness; depleted and spent. The others disappeared into the blackness of the night. One single golden feather floated softly to the ground.

Exhausted, Edric and Maawan fell into the ring.

Nothing could be spoken. No one wanted to break the spell. With little understanding of what they had just observed, each of them looked up to the sky, or lifted their hands in the air, gesturing their assumption that the gods had spoken. Bianna watched their reaction, as her inner voice assented.

'What we have witnessed is linked not only to the future of Edric and Maawan, but to Brigantia and Albion,' she thought. Then she rushed to the side of the fallen Dugall.

Maawan picked up the feather and touched it to her lips, placing it in her hair for safe keeping.

CHAPTER TEN

Avowal
Declaration

B IANNA GATHERED THE HORSES and led them down the hill, following the three warriors who carried Dugall to the camp at the farmstead of Epicus. He was breathing but weakened by his shift-mutation. Camulo led the way. Dyn, walking and stumbling at the side of the fallen Druid, spoke healing chants over him. Edric and Maawan followed behind, hand in hand.

They did not talk, as the experience of the dusk sun was too much for either of them to understand, let alone put into words. They knew they must be together, but for now the talking could wait.

That night, they slept together in the roundhouse barn belonging to Epicus. Their love making was long and tender; urgent, and desperate. Edric caressed every part of Maawan's body, enjoying the movements she made, as she moaned with delight at his touch.

'This night is the night the gods have ordained for me,' she thought, as she gave herself willingly to her lover.

Edric pulled her closer, sweeping her into his embrace. He kissed her open lips eagerly; delicately touching her body while he savoured her mouth. He felt the softness of her skin as he moved his hands to embrace her breasts. His finger traced the circle of her nipples. He watched as they rose and tightened. Slowly he moved to kiss her secret parts, showing her how much he had longed for her.

The night stretched out, and the lovers slept little.

When slumber came, it was deep and dreamless.

The sun shone through the cracks in the barn walls as Edric woke. He remained still, his mind mulling over the experience of the night before. He savoured every moment, as he looked at the beautiful girl in his arms. Her golden red hair fell softly over the blanket. He watched the rise and fall of her chest as each breath flowed in and out. To Edric, it felt as if a small bird had landed in his hand, and the responsibility to nurture and care for this delicate creature was his. He had never known the weight of love before. It seemed almost overwhelming. He found himself shedding silent tears of joy. 'Could life get any better?' he asked himself.

Maawan opened her eyes. The first thing she saw was Edric smiling at her. She smiled back. At first, she didn't remember where he had come from or what he was doing there.

'The portal to the Otherworld must have opened and I had passed through,' she thought. She had felt the power of the opening the eve before, as she danced among the stones in the twilight. Questions danced through her mind, but they did not find a settling place, and she didn't want to chase the answers. Her soul told her that this was where she was meant to be.

But she wondered, 'Is my own soul deceived?' She could feel the dark edges of her mind spreading slowly into a realisation that she dared not be honest with Edric. She felt sick at the thought. Dismissing the feelings, she moved to get up, but Edric pulled her back and once again, he took her. Softly he whispered into her ear, kissing as he spoke.

'My princess Maawan, I have been waiting all my life for you.' Maawan responded with a smile. He touched her nose and her eye lids with soft kisses as he whispered again, 'I would like you to become my lady. Will you give me your hand?'

Maawan turned away. 'Lord, I would. With every part of my being, I would be yours.' Edric sensed a reticence in her reply; that she had more to say. He wanted the morning to continue for ever, so he did not press her further.

They lay together until time to break the fast was over, and the sun was at its zenith. Bianna was the first to venture to the doorway of the barn. She coughed to warn them that she was there. 'Edric, we need to talk. Can you come?' she asked.

'I will be there shortly, Bian,' Edric responded.

The group was sitting a short distance away. They had begun to discuss the Sith of what they had seen. Dugall had improved through the night and was deep in conversation with Dyn. Dyn wanted to know more about the shape shifting that Dugall was clearly able perform. Dugall wanted to know about the younger Druid's journey with Maawan and Camulo. The three warriors were questioning Camulo about his role guarding Maawan.

Questions flew from one to the other. Stories unfolded, shedding some light onto the mystery besetting them. But one thing they were resigned to; last night they saw the gods at work joining two people in power and in love. It was Dugall who went to the barn next.

'Edric. We need to talk. Please come and join us,' he entreated.

Shortly after, Edric joined the boodle, who by this time was again sharing meat. Edric realised he was very hungry, but thoughtful of Maawan, he took some cold slices of salted beef, some nuts and roots, and a flagon of water into the barn. The grin on his face told the company that his return might be a little while longer.

When Edric re-appeared, it was with Maawan on his arm. She looked coy, as the faces meeting her smiled, and nodded to each other with knowing nods.

'Bianna, we need some explanations about last night,' declared Edric. 'What happened out there?' he quizzed.

'I don't know,' answered Bianna truthfully. 'And I have grave concerns about the shadow we saw, and what happened to Dugall. There are signs and omens for us to study, but I believe that the gods were involved. This was not a chance meeting. There is reason at work here.'

'Well, I know this.' smiled Edric, making light of Bianna's concerns. 'I have found my wife and I am the happiest man alive.'

'Can we go home then?' asked Wulfnud eagerly. 'That shadow gave me the *uabhais*. The queen has gone south. You have found your bride. Now surely, we can go home,' he pronounced.

'I have a few questions for Camulo first,' said Edric, without committing to an answer. He turned to Camulo. 'Why are you with Maawan?'

Camulo responded by asking, 'Why are you calling her Maawan?'

Edric admitted that he didn't know her real name, but she had called herself Maawan Biann when he first met her. She was nothing but a servant girl, with a sharp wit. He explained that he had just rescued her from the clutches of a tyrant, and she was out to impress him. He glanced at Maawan and smiled as he teased her.

Camulo continued, 'Then the little one came to me. I chose to travel with her as she journeyed north. She had lost her mistress and set out to find her. But Milburga can answer for herself. Tell them,

Milburga.' Camulo also looked toward Maawan. His eyes were soft and gentle, as he smiled at her. Maawan realised that once again, she had woven trouble for herself. She sat among her friends and her enemies. Worse still, she had slept with an enemy, whom she loved. She thought quickly, understanding that she might lose her lover if she told the truth, but she might also lose her head. Maawan lied.

'Edric, I am sorry I told you my name was Maawan. I am Milburga, just as Camulo told you.'

'Aah,' beamed Edric, showing pleasure at this news. 'I don't care what your name is. I love you. Even if your name was *Cailleach,* I would still love you. I want you to become my wife.' Maawan looked away while he spoke.

Camulo spun his head round to watch Maawan's reaction to this confession. Smiling to himself, and nodding his head, he thought, 'I knew! I knew it. Did I not see it in her eyes? Did it not tell in her movements? I was reminded of the little girl Reagan and I cared for all those years ago…the look in her eyes when she asked about Eachann. Did I not see last night, a mirror reflecting Cartimandua and Eachann? I am certain now.' His thoughts racing, Camulo, looked directly at Edric, and asked, 'My lord, are you the queen's man or Venutius'?'

Edric, placing his hand on the hilt of his dagger, cautiously answered. 'I am a man of the people; a Brigante through and through. My politics have no place here, on this day,' he responded. For the safety of his princess, Camulo calmly looked at Edric, and smiled.

'I also am a Brigante through and through. We are on the same side, my friend.'

'Then we will be friends, Camulo. You have protected my woman, and for that I am grateful. Journey with us. We will be glad to have you among us.'

Both men grabbed the wrist of the other in friendship. They slapped each other on the back, for good measure.

The following morning, they set off back to Gabrantovices.

They again travelled under cover. The route they chose for their return to Gabrantovices took them back toward Ellestob, over open moorland. As they rode over the moors along the ridge toward the valley, Buite, who was travelling a little way in front of the others, turned with urgency.

'Edric, there are soldiers below us. They are camping as the crow flies. I can see the standard of Rome.' Edric and Buite sped toward the ridge where they could see beyond the flat moorland to the encampment. There was no hiding for them; just a hope that any Roman look-out, had not seen them.

They turned back to stop the others approaching further, hoping they had time to re-route to avoid confrontation. Within moments, they heard the Cornu and a rally call. Soldiers mounted their horses and made for the place they had spotted Edric and Buite. Dugall and Dyn began to work together on an 'invocation of hiding.' Bianna called up the Druid fog. The warriors prepared for a fight. Bianna, Maawan and Dyn stayed behind the warriors.

The six warriors stood their ground. A brume had risen over the top of the ridge. It spread thickly across the moorland. As the soldiers advanced, the fog was so thick that they could not see beyond the first few arms' lengths. Edric and Camulo lunged forward, to meet the first soldiers. With clean swipes, their heads rolled. Three more soldiers followed, and three more heads rolled. Before they could take their breath, another six appeared in front of them. Each took one, fighting for their lives. The soldiers went down hard. Buite was outnumbered as three soldiers stumbled on him in the misty confusion. Beored was right by his side, slicing and stabbing in frenzy. Two fell. One continued to retaliate. Camulo was swift as he leapt to Beored's defence. His long sword cut deeply through the enemy's neck. Edric covered Wulfnud as he attacked two more of the Latins as they hit the ridge edge. One rolled back on his horse, and the steed stumbled on the rocky *brycg*. He lost his footing as Dugall's sword ripped into the chest of the rider.

'How many more?' called Edric.

Bianna, seeing the picture in her mind's eye, called back. 'Seven. I see seven!' she continued lifting her arms, circling to thicken the foggy confusion.

Dugall shouted 'One!' as he sliced the leg off another.

'Two!' shouted Wulfnud, followed by Buite and Beored simultaneously shouting, 'Three!'

Camulo and Edric lined up and waited. The last three soldiers appeared on the ridge and divided in three ways. Edric chased after the middle soldier, slaughtering him easily. Camulo chased the right-hand soldier. The fog was thicker now, and even Camulo struggled to see the rider. But there he was, right in front of him. With one swipe, the Galea helmet crashed to the ground. The horse bolted, crashing into the horse of the last soldier, knocking him off his steed. Edric, as quick as lightning, dismounted and stood over him. His sword went deep, cutting through the heart.

'Seven,' he called.

Twenty-four bodies lay before the Brigante. Edric walked to the edge of the scarp and looked to the campus below. Four or five people could be spotted, but they were busy in retreat. Edric could see no danger from them.

They laid the dead soldiers in a row. They took the pins and badges and anything that might be of value, before Dugall offered their remains as a sacrifice to Taranis and any animal in need of food. They decided to make their way to Ellestob before night fall. Camulo led the way.

The old hag was in her place, sitting by the bridgeway as they approached Ellestob.

Maawan was pleased to be back, and Camulo was even more pleased. He rushed to his home, calling for Raegan. Before long, the village was alive with people welcoming the travellers.

That night, the fires were lit in the houses, with beds made for every one of the visitors. A welcome feast was laid before them; with as much rye beer and mead as that they could drink. Maawan and Edric stayed with Camulo and Raegan, while Dugall, Bianna, and Dyn settled down in the neighbouring home of the two sept Druids. The warrior cadre also settled for the night in the homes of the Ellestob. As the night drew in, the snow fell. Silently and deeply, it fell, until the world became cloaked in white.

Travel was now impossible. The only option to Edric was to stay at Ellestob until the weather improved. Frustration kicked at his mind, like a horse kicking at a stable door. He longed to take his bride home to Gabrantovices for the festival of Imbolc. He was also aware that he needed to be home to steer to fruition the plans to join Venutius. Sharing the breakfast table with his host, he decided to make the most of the captivity.

'Camulo, may I ask?' He nodded for Edric to continue. 'I see all around me the spoils of your practices as a warrior. I saw your action yesterday out on the ridge. It made me wonder to whom you were joined.'

Camulo had anticipated this question and had already decided that honesty was the best course of action. 'I was in the royal household, working for both the queen and Venutius before they divorced. I did not want to stand against either of them when their marriage ended and decided that my work with them was finished. I retired here, to Ellestob some years ago.'

Edric bit his bottom lip momentarily as he puzzled over this answer.

'This is a fair explanation,' he thought, tapping his lip with his fingers. 'Camulo would be a good ally.'

He dropped his hand and offered it to Camulo. 'Will you work with us, Camulo?' he asked.

'For the sake of Milburga, I will,' he said. Edric was pleased with this answer.

Maawan smiled to herself.

Just then, the blanket across the doorway was moved to one side as Bianna and Dugall entered. They bowed to Edric and Maawan and nodded to Camulo and Raegan, who was sitting by the fire.

'Greetings, this white morning,' welcomed Camulo. 'Join us by the fire,' he said, pointing to a bench. 'I hope you slept well.' Bianna nodded, and Dugall sat by her side. Raegan offered fruit from the wooden bowl then pointed to another large bowl full of nuts. She indicated for them to take whatever they wanted. Dugall smiled at the ring of friends.

'We slept very well, though we have much to think about and discuss. It is clear that we will not be able to travel until the weather warms a little, so I hope that our presence will not hinder your home plans, Camulo.'

'The snow is deep, and the freezing wind blows across the land. You are welcome to stay until the snow has gone,' he answered. Dyn entered the room, looking sheepish.

'I wondered if I might join you,' he asked, looking at Maawan, as if her response would work the magic that allowed him to sit in the inner circle. Maawan read his face and smiled.

'Come. Come, gentle Dyn,' she said, and moved along the bench to make a space for him to sit by her side. 'Dyn, I have something to ask you,' Maawan continued. 'I would like it very much if you would become my Druid. I would like you to be by my side as I learn the skills of defence and attack. Camulo has promised to teach me, and I would welcome your support.'

Dyn looked round the room, unable to take in his good fortune. Dugall leaned toward Dyn and smiled.

'I agree, Dyn. This feels right for you and Edric's woman.' The others agreed also, and so Dyn stood to thank them all as he took on his new position.

'Sing for us, Dyn,' requested Maawan, so Dyn began to sing in a lilting melody, as the group sat round the fire, thinking their own thoughts:

FIRES OF BRIGANTIA

'Soft is the earth as she sleeps,
Covered in cloak of pure white.
But under the cover grows the white rose,
With fire; a sacred birth right.
Tomorrow the fight will be fought.
Brigg's children will fight in the war.
But Brigga will rise from the battlefield,
Wielding truth, that freedom may soar.'

Edric turned once more to Camulo. 'You are a warrior Camulo,' he said, pointing to the trophies hanging around the house. 'Yet you have a gentle spirit?' he questioned.

'I have seen what war does, Edric. And I have felt what peace is like. We fight for what we know; for what we believe in. So do the Romans. They are fighting for their faith and their country. They believe they are right to fight. They believe they are bringing us a 'better life'.'

Camulo fell silent for a while, and then added, 'Can't we all be right? Our queen brought peace; one without bloodshed. The blood is spilled by her own people, opposed to the changes she longs to bring to her people.'

Edric asked, 'But at what cost? Our ways; our Druidic faith; our country—gone! All gone to foreigners who destroy and kill in the name of their gods. They take our land and our gods; they rape our women and kill our children.'

'Yes, Edric. It is true, for those who oppose them. But ask yourself this: if change is inevitable, should we not embrace it for the sake of peace? Through change, hardships, and loss, we learn to grow. We are on the cusp of such a time now, but our faith and beliefs teach us that there is a season for everything. The season of new growth, fullness, and blossoming is followed by a season of withering and death. All are necessary before the next life cycle can begin again. It is the circle of our belief.'

Dugall joined into the conversation. 'I hate what the Romans are doing in our land. I hate it! I hate what they are doing to our people. They take our best men and make them slaves. With whose authority? I promised to avenge these wrongs, and I will continue to do so, till my breath is no more. But our faith cannot be destroyed, Edric. It is eternal. We live by the sun and the moon, and their perpetual cycles. We depend on these rhythms. The flowering of the earth, the movement of the seasons, and patterns for life are built round these constants. These things live, whether we believe in them or not.'

'Our beliefs; that each death brings forth new life; that each springtime brings forth promise of harvest — these beliefs live in our hearts and our souls,' Camulo added.

'And though we may question these certainties in the darkest of nights, we see they are renewed with each new sunrise. You know these things, Edric. Each and every one of us, knows this. You may change your words, but what is in your heart remains the same. It is that which makes us who we are. No matter what life brings, or what changes may be thrust upon us in our world; the sun, the moon, and the stars above us, will still be there, long after we have been laid to rest.' To demonstrate the depth of his feeling, Dugall thumped his chest and his heart.

'I have much to think about,' said Edric.

'I like the peacemaker, Camulo,' he thought, 'but I know that my own fight has not yet been won, neither on the field of battle nor in my head.'

As the snow continued to fall, the company became increasingly restless. Hemmed in on all sides by the frozen vapour that was quickly turning to ice, they knew that taking the horses onto the glassy surface was asking for trouble. Patience was needed, and something to occupy their restless spirits. Maawan began to think about her plan to learn the art of battle, so as soon as she could, she approached Camulo.

'I have an idea, Camulo. Would it be possible to dig the snow from the green circle in the village and make it into a ring for battle training? We could ask the village men to help with the clearing, and then organise some vying between them. Maybe we could have a feast day to bring the women together too,' she pleaded. Raegan, who was listening, thought it was a brilliant idea, and encouraged Camulo to allow it.

'Yes, indeed,' he agreed. 'I will get the men to start clearing the snow and ice. It will be good work for them, little one.'

The very next day, the men gathered in the ring made of wooden benches and began to create a good fighting arena. Buite, Beored, and Wulfnud were eager to join in the preparations, and the fighting. The children joined in too, and a sense of fun and laughter overtook the sept. The women began to prepare for a day of eating and drinking, over and above their usual daily supplies. They were amazed by how much food they had amassed, even after a long hard winter.

Bianna joined the group of women as they laughed and gossiped, while preparing for the feast. She listened as they spoke of their love for their warrior leader, Camulo, and for the 'little one,' whom he had taken under his protection. Bianna listened as they told stories of blessings that had come to the sept when Milburga joined them.

Bianna could see why they had grown to love her. She had begun to feel the same way too.

But the vision of Maawan wearing a crown of stars on her head still brought consternation to Bianna. It was a mystery she did not fully understand. She had wanted to speak to Edric upon their mother's death, but no opportunity had arisen.

'And now it was too late. Edric is betrothed to Maawan or Milburga, or whatever she calls herself,' thought Bianna. She reminded herself of the purpose of their travels; the gods had ordained that she must protect Maawan. But one thing she purposed to do; ask some questions of Maawan directly, and in secret.

It was almost two full moons before the snow began to thaw and the sun came out of hibernation. Imbolc had come and gone. The fun day at Ellestob ran into a week of sparring and contending amongst the men and warriors in the sept, and eclipsed the spring festival, when it finally showed its face.

During that time Camulo had worked with Maawan to show her the rudiments of defence. Edric had sparred with her too, helping to build the warrior spirit in his little bird. But each time she had come against him, trying her moves of defence, Edric had picked her up and kissed her.

'Edric, I am trying here, to be serious.' Her grave face showed annoyance as she pushed him away. But Edric just kissed her more, and more urgently with each push she gave him, until she was locked into his arms with no chance of escape.

'One day, Edric Beorand, one day,' she swore, 'One day I will be a warrior, and it will be no thanks to you,' she laughed. The contesting among the warriors and working men in the sept brought a sense of relief and rather than enemies, many friendships were made. The week had ended with dancing and drinking, and the hope that winter would be over in the not-too-distant future.

Bianna woke to a bright light streaming through her door. Dugall had risen early and gone to the shrine with offerings of beer and the dregs from the night before. She lay a little while longer, drifting into and out of sleep. She loved this time in between when reality stands a way off, and the otherworld beckons.

She allowed her mind to float away, half awake, half dreaming, seeing the green cliffs of home and the blue sea beyond Gabrantovices. Dugall was by her side, holding her safely as they stood on the cliff edge. She was holding a baby in her arms and rocking gently, swaying from side to side as she cradled the child. Suddenly, revealed to her mind's eye, she saw the sacred isle of Ynys Môn rising from the sea. Druids were running in fear all across the coastal edge. Dugall took the child from her and held her close. She wept; overpowered by grief and a sense of loss she did not understand. As she watched, she saw flames falling from the sky, burning the island; Druids running, trying to hide from the raging inferno. It was too much.

'No…' she called out. 'NO!' she shouted. Dugall came running into the house.

'What is it, Bianna?' He ran to grab her and hold her. She wept uncontrollably.

'I have seen the end, Dugall. I have seen the terrible end,' she wept.

CHAPTER ELEVEN

CHAOS
Disarray

Packing the horses ready for travel was the easy part. Leaving Ellestob behind was harder.

The entire village turned out to wish them farewell, knowing that this could so easily be the last time they would meet. There were promises passed from one group to another, and offers of help, should they ever be in need. Each step away was a heavy one, until Ellestob was out of sight, and the sun lay before them. East, they travelled, as swift as hawks flying for their prey.

Approaching Gabrantovices, they saw a pillar of smoke rising against the weak spring sun. Edric sent Wulfnud ahead to report. That night as they camped, they swore by Taranis that if anything had happened to their people, they would take the revenge without a thought.

'I vow before my god that I will take pleasure in spilling the guts of any of them,' swore Beored. He swung his fist in the air, looking for his friends to agree their support.

Buite took out his dagger, and in a gesture, stabbed at the air, twisting the knife, as if he was twisting the giblets from a stomach. 'They would not dare to harm my sisters,' he said as he looked round the faces of warriors sitting by the fire. But a hint of doubt leaked from the tone of his voice, and a silence followed. Edric tried not to worry, making light-hearted fun out of the situation. But worry he did.

A flicker of a ghostly batwing; a voyeur of death, darted across his vision, discharging unease. Each made a bed for the night. Dread sat with them, snatching sleep away.

When Wulfnud returned, it was with a heavy heart. He looked physically shaken, as he dismounted his steed. The colour had drained from his cheeks, and his hands trembled as he spoke.

'The sept has been razed Edric,' he reported. 'The Roman ensign stands in the village circle and the Druid grove is decimated.'

'Oh, my gods! What have they done? What have they done?' sobbed Bianna, as the dream of the fires and desolation came flooding back into her mind. She started to shake. Her legs weakened. Dugall came to her side, hugging her tightly, giving comfort and support.

Maawan, with outstretched arms, stepped toward the two. Wrapping her arms round them both, she joined with Bianna in lament, as tears flowing down their cheeks through choking sobs.

Buite sank to the ground, his head in his hands.

'What of the Druids?' asked Dugall. 'Any survivors?'

'I do not know,' answered Wulfnud.

'Where are the Romans now, Wulfnud?' Edric asked.

'They have left. There are bodies strewn around the village. It is devastation, Edric. Death holds the land.' Wulfnud hung his head, as he tried to contain his emotion. Edric called to Beored, who immediately jumped upright, in response.

'Go! Take Buite. Fetch Camulo; be swift. Ask him to bring as many men as he can. We will camp near here until we have full understanding of the situation. Go!'

The remainder searched for a place to make camp while they decided on a course of action. They found a spot just a few miles away from the sept, near enough to make a safe trip to the village, but far enough away to be hidden. Down the narrow tree lined track, the convoy rambled until the ravine opened out into a flat area overlooking a fosse; the depth of at least four men.

The area was hidden deep in the wood and would give not only shelter, but some obscurity from anyone approaching. Once settled and feeling more secure, Dugall and Edric ventured toward Gabrantovices, to assess the situation.

Discreetly they approached the sept, realising that the decimation must have occurred within the last daylight. They drew their swords and rode into the sept. Nothing stirred. The Roman ensign had been staked in the middle of the green.

Edric dismounted and with one swipe, grabbed the ensign and broke it over his knee. He threw the emblem into the ashes of one of the fires still smouldering across the village.

Dugall had dismounted and was walking quietly toward the Druid grove. For a moment he was out of Edric's sight, but minutes later Edric heard him talking and went to find him.

Three Druids had come to meet him. They had been hiding in the wood by the side of the shrine. One began to speak urgently.

'There were about twenty of them. They came from nowhere, without warning. They had fire already in their hands, throwing the wands into the houses as they stampeded through. We were so busy trying to put the fires out, we did not see them coming back. With drawn swords, they killed whoever was in their way.'

'What about Gedrae and Ric?' asked Dugall. 'They were warriors as well as priests. Where are they?'

Boreus emerged from the Druid hut. He was holding his arm, blood still flowing from a deep cut. 'Ric is slaughtered, Dugall. In the heap, by the lord's house,' he said, indicating with elbow and nose toward the roundhouse belonging to Edric. 'They tried to defend against them, but the rush was so swift, they did not stand a chance. Ric died defending our homes. Some escaped, including Gedrae, I think. Others are hiding in their houses or at the back of the cairn beyond. Some fled to the bay.'

Edric made his way to the green again, this time calling loudly to his people.

'Good people of Gabrantovices. Come to me. I am your Lord Edric. Though I am found wanting, I am here now. Wherever you are, come to me. We will make this our home again. We will not let the murdering Romans win.' The first to come out of hiding were Maccar and Cerdic. Both were wounded. Blood covered Maccar's priestly cloak as he limped toward the clearing. Cerdic had a shoulder wound which prevented him from carrying his sword or shield. He was bruised around his face and body. Edric signalled for someone to fetch a bench, and the two sat.

'What of our armoury, Maccar? Did they find our weapons?'

'No, lord. The weapons are safe. The Romans came like the wind and left just as swiftly. They did not stop to survey the sept,' answered Maccar. One by one, people showed themselves. Two here, one there, a few together; slowly they came toward the green. Osma and Yetta, clinging to each other, came forward, crying and wailing all the while.

'What is the damage to your homes?' asked Edric. 'How many homes can be salvaged?' The people ran round the village assessing the damage. They counted the dead, dragging the bodies into the circle. Edric's head bowed low as he saw the extent of the killings. Sadness and anger filled his heart.

'Each family must find their loved ones and separate them, so we might see who is missing, and who is still with us,' ordered Edric. 'We must first see our families and friends into their passing to the Otherworld. Then we can — we *will* — rebuild!' he vowed.

'Lord, I've found one alive: a roman.' A shout from one of the farm workers called the attention of the crowd. 'Found him cowering in the long grass, by the gate. He was trying to get away. He'd fallen from his horse.'

Edric drew his sword, ready to behead the captive Roman, but Gedrae went to stop him.

'My lord, is it not best we find out what he knows and where the troop came from before his life is ended?' he asked. Edric dropped his sword, giving himself time to digest this idea.

'Tie him up and gag him. Put him in the shelter in the pig pen, with the other pigs. I will come to him later,' Edric ordered, spitting on the man as he spoke.

Dugall went to fetch the others back from the camp, leaving a track for Camulo and the warriors to follow back to Gabrantovices, though he guessed that Buite and Beored would know to come home.

Bianna went straight to her mother's room to see what damage had been done. Yetta was at the door waiting. She flung herself at Bianna. 'Oh! Bianna. It's terrible. The roof has gone. But I am so pleased to see you.' She grabbed Bianna again and clung to her as if her life depended on it.

'You have done well, Yetta. Are you wounded at all?' asked Bianna.

'No, we are fine, but Osma will not stop crying.'

'The shock of it will ease, Yetta. Give it time,' comforted Bianna.

She looked at the damaged home. The roof would need replacing, but she found the furnishings and beds could be salvaged. She scoured the rest of the house, making note of the things necessary to get it into a living state again.

That night, those not wounded by the onslaught began to clear the damaged roof of the nobleman's home and repair it. It would only be a temporary fix, but it would keep the weather out, at least. The Great Hall was filled to capacity with as many homeless as they could fit. Edric took charge, introducing a plan to build back the homes that had been destroyed. He asked Cerdic to oversee the project using his skills as a constructor.

Two evenings later, Camulo arrived with nine others. They were incensed by the destruction, having seen nothing like it in Ellestob. Camulo offered his help in any way and promised to stay until at least the following spring. His men began to build a pyre on the cairn beyond.

The sacred shrine had been left untouched by the Roman devastation. The bodies of loved ones were covered, each with his own cloak. One by one the families carried their kinsmen to the pyre. Dugall led the procession.

Family by family, they laid the bodies atop the pyre. There was much weeping. Edric spoke to the crowd gathered there, but found he had but few words to give. He wanted to encourage his people, to show his love for them and his grief for their loss, but the words stuck in his throat.

Maawan moved close to him. She held his hand and squeezed it a little, hoping to infuse courage. She whispered, 'Edric, tell them of your love and loss. Just say it,' she suggested.

Edric found he could not stop the tears that were running down his cheeks and chin.

'My people of Gabrantovices. This is a day of great loss. We are in a time of great change, and before the end is decided in this battle of ours, we find we have been thrust into a time of chaos and great upheaval.' Pointing to the pyre he continued. 'Such is the chaos that we see before us now; such that we see our own people sacrificed in the barter.' Taking time to wipe his eyes, Edric continued, although he had no idea what he was saying or whether the people understood or received it. His grief was so deep as to be unbearable. 'We battle against a mighty enemy, and others will lose their lives also. This is too much,' he said. He fell to the ground and wailed to the gods. 'This is too much!' He shook his fist at whatever gods were listening. Thumping the ground and wailing. Each person there fell also to the ground and following Edric in drumming the earth. An almighty thunder rose from the anguish expressed. Then silence.

Bianna rose. She raised her arms high and looked toward the heavens.

'The souls of our own will rise in the fire. They will join the good earth again. Their lives will not be in vain. The gods hear our agony, and we will come through this mayhem to find a different day,' she promised. Lighting the fire, the people walked slowly round the pyre, offering whatever gift they could to their loved ones for the passage from this life to the next.

Dagger in hand, and with Camulo by his side, Edric placed his foot on the shoulder of the Roman, as he sat cowering in the corner of the pig shed.

'What orders did you hold and from whom?' asked Camulo.

The Roman did not speak. With a strong push, Edric knocked the soldier until he rolled onto his side. The ties holding him caused him to overbalance and his head hit the floor. Edric put his foot on the soldier's head, pressing hard into his temple, and held his dagger to the hostage's throat.

'You have been asked a question,' Edric said, repeating Camulo's words.

As the dagger pressed into the jugum, the prisoner spluttered. 'We were on a raid; no one sent us. We had been told by one of your own that this area was leaderless.'

'Then who is the traitor in our sept?' questioned Camulo.

Edric moved his dagger down to the hands of the captive, choosing the right-hand thumb, he sliced it off, tossing it toward the pigs. Screams of pain were lost among the squealing pigs as they snuffled for the morsel.

'Tell us who,' Edric shouted.

'I don't know. I am but a numerus in the Roman army. I didn't get to know any of it,' he said, pleading for leniency. Edric picked off the other thumb, spreading it out, ready to slice.

With desperate urgency the soldier cried, 'He was one of yours, I swear. I never saw him, but there was talk of his prowess. They spoke of many victories in battle, calling him 'The Green Man.' The soldier continued to plead, hoping that this little piece of information would allay further pain. Camulo touched Edric's arm, holding him from further torture.

Edric walked away. Camulo sent a Druid to bind the Roman's wounded hand and move him from the pigs. Still tied, he was dragged to a warmer shelter and left with a guard watching his every move. Osma was tasked with feeding him once a day. The guard was ordered to kill him should he attempt to escape.

Edric ordered a search of all the homes, with instruction to let him know if they should find any green woven cloaks or cape.

During the next six months, the people worked to rebuild the settlement, with improvements where needed. The Romans did not return, but for extra security, the walls around the sept were strengthened and a permanent watch was begun. The gate to the sept was doubly secured. When the warriors and fighting men had healed from their wounds, they rode as outriders traversing the coastal road. They circled westward then southward, looking for any sign of soldiers in the area. It seemed that, as swiftly as the mercenaries had appeared, they disappeared into the morning mist.

Edric, never far from wondering who the traitor might be, visited the captive soldier, intending further questioning, and torture if necessary. He planned on learning something of the ways of the Romans to use in tactical battle against them.

'What is your name, pig?' Edric kicked the soldier in the thigh, as he spoke.

'I am Lucius Manius; a servant of Claudius, lord and god of Rome.'

Edric kicked him again, ignoring his statements. 'Tell me where you were camped?' demanded Edric, holding his sword loosely by his side.

The Roman answered honestly, fearing that Edric's sword might easily find another place to hang. 'I camped inside the border of Parisii. I have lived there for some years. The Four Kings of Parisi have treaties with Claudius, so I live there; called only when needed.'

'If you are settled there, why did you come to us, killing our people, and destroying our lands?'

'We were told you belonged to Venutius. The legatus legionis ordered us to kill any rebel forces.'

'Who told you about us? Who was the traitor you spoke of?' Edric pursued.

'One of your own, my lord. That is all I know. I never saw him, but he had a reputation for being a solitary man and parsimonious in his dealings. He made a living from the forest, curing and selling coney, I understand, but that is all I know,'

'Then you must know his name,' insisted Edric, once more laying the soldier's fingers flat, as if preparing to cut a few off.

'I do not, my lord,' the soldier pleaded. 'But his appellative, I believe, is 'The Green Cloak of Donn'— Donn Gearr.'

Edric believed that Lucius Manus knew little more than he had already divulged, but each day Edric went to question him.

Each day, Edric learned a little more about the Romans. Each day Edric challenged this captive soldier about his way of life and faith. He questioned him about his homelands and family.

Each day Osma came with food, and sat listening to Edric's questions, and the answers given. Each day she found herself spending more and more time with the Roman soldier.

The building work continued, alongside the working of the land, gleaning whatever they could toward harvest and grain storing. The hunting and fishing saw lean supplies but nevertheless, they were able to stockpile enough foodstuffs to ward off any concerns about starvation.

Camulo's men joined in with the hard labour, fetching and cutting the long straw and combed wheat needed for the roofs. So once again, Samheim called.

Maawan had settled into the sept. Edric introduced her to his people as 'my lady Milburga,' and she began to get to know them, and love them. Life began to regain its way. Edric had decided that he would take 'Milburga's' hand in marriage, a seal of his love for her, and a reason to celebrate once again. Happiness had crept back into his life, and Maawan was the main reason. He found he could not function without her smile. He loved the happiness she exuded and loved the way she felt when he wrapped his arms round her.

He was pleased also that his sister Bianna had come to care for the gentle ways of the red-haired girl, spending time together laughing and talking. He told her of his pleasure, knowing that Maawan was accepted.

Bianna confessed, 'Although I do not yet understand why the gods expect me to protect this servant girl, still; I find myself questioning less each day. I trust the gods will show the way in all these circumstances. Maawan is like a sister to me now.'

As the two women walked together to the river to wash blankets, Bianna tripped, tumbling down over the blankets as she dropped them. Whether she banged her head or whether the gods struck her, a rainbow appeared before her as she lost all sense of the world.

Maawan called for Dugall. 'Come quickly. It's Bianna,' she shouted. Dugall lifted her onto the blankets, making a pillow for her head. Blood gushed from a gash on her brow. 'Bianna,' called Dugall as he began to weave a healing spell. 'I call to the gods of healing,' he said as he circled his hands in front of the injury. 'Fetch water, Maawan, and fetch my herbs; bring Lus, torranian, and the figwort. I will need it as a salve for her wound.' Maawan dashed off to fetch the medicines, while Dugall prayed to Brighid Verbeia, goddess of healing.

Bianna began to call out in a state of confusion, 'Brighid, Brighid…pains…child. Much fire…Imbolc, full moon…caul and seawaters…the gods! The gods!' she called out as if giving birth herself. Dugall and Maawan stroked her head, trying to bring comfort, before settling her in the warmth of the blankets. Dugall spread the herbal balm over the bloody cut and carried Bianna back to the grove. Her ramblings continued into the night.

The day Edric asked for the hand of Maawan for the second time, she was washing clothes in the stream by the sheep pens. He followed her out there, as she carried the woven bag full of the smell of Edric and their love. She placed the cloth on a stone in the water and began pounding it.

Edric sat with his feet in the stream, splashing and paddling like a child. Maawan laughed, but the more she laughed, the higher the splashes, until she was as wet as if she had laid in the flow.

'Will you marry me now, Princess Maawan? Since we met, we have been together, living and loving. It is time to ask for the blessing of the gods.'

Maawan had thought many times about how she might give answer to this question. Her decision had swung back and forth until she was dizzy with the whole idea. She wanted so much to be with him, and felt so safe in his hands, but dread sat on her shoulder.

'What if he found out who I really am? How would he feel about me then?' she troubled.

When Edric asked, she was taken by surprise. Without thinking, she had flung her arms round his neck and agreed.

As Yule arrived, the sept was ready to embrace the new Lady of Gabrantovices. Holly, winter branches of yew, and berries had been laced all around the village. Candles and torches were placed to give a soft but bright light. An archway full of winter roses and mistletoe framed the walk through the Druid grove to a place beyond the sept, overlooking the sea.

Warriors on horseback holding torches of fire lined the way. Dugall, wearing his priestly white cloak, held the hand of Bianna, also in white, as they led the procession to the cupola covered sacred circle on the hilltop. Dyn followed, singing a marching song, as a band of other fellows followed with bone pipes and *carnyx*, drums, and tambourines. Behind the musicians, Maccar and Gedrae waved *feys* dipped in holy water, scented with pine and red berries.

Then Edric, smiling from cheek to cheek, walked to the inner circle.

FIRES OF BRIGANTIA

His long cloak of red, fastened with a bronze filigree fibula at the shoulder, swung from side to side, matching the beat of the music. His tunic was red also, though his braccae had been woven of a mix of red, blue, and green. He wore his father's belt and sword and had on his finger the signet ring of Bloodeworthe. He tied his hair into a topknot, adding the wheel of Taranis painted in woad to the back of his neck. He walked with his shoulders straight and his head high. He nodded to his people as he passed through the crowd. When all were assembled, a single rhythm drumbeat began, signalling the entrance of the bride.

Camulo walked at the side of Maawan as she entered the circle, each of her steps echoing the beat of the drum. The crowd gasped when they saw Maawan sweeping down the centre of the circle: her long red hair hung loosely, cascading round her shoulders. The red fabric of her dress, caught up on each shoulder and fastened with a gold brooch and drawn together tightly round her slim waist by a gold-coloured belt. On her head was a garland of holly and ivy, intertwined with berries and winter roses. At the front of the winter crown, a single golden feather was fixed. In the candlelight it shone as a beacon toward heaven. The berries glistened as a myriad of stars. Over one arm, Maawan held a soft white cape lined with fur: a gift from Bianna. She walked toward Edric calmly and regally.

Dugall reached for Maawan's hand and, taking it, drew her toward Edric. Edric took her hand, kissing it gently as she turned toward him. There in the candlelight, Dugall called to the four winds and the Fires of Brigga to bless this union. The warm flickering light seemed to move in rhythm to the *caim* that Dugall uttered. Holding his arms wide to the crowd and to the couple standing before him, he nodded towards Maawan and Edric.

'Today, I bestow on you, new names, to carry you forward into your future together.' Looking first at Maawan, then at Edric, he styled new titles for each, as a sign of his personal blessing. 'Lady of the White Rose, and Lord of the Horse Spirits; may you always bear a spirit of freedom, and love. May you always be revealed to those who care for you and be hidden from your enemies. For as long as the Spirit of Brigantia rests on you, may life be long and blessed.'

Edric took the white fur lined cloak from Maawan's arm and wrapped it around her shoulders. Maawan met his gaze and clearly, she began to sing:

*Like winter snow poured through the gates
That separates our worlds,*

110

Your lovely soft enveloping
Calls; whispers through the folds.
And once again we touch, embrace.
Two hands meet and grasp.
And all things in-between our worlds
Vanish in the clasp.'

Led by Dyn, the people began to walk round the stone circle, as they had done each time a sacred ceremony took place. They invoked the Brigante Well of Wisdom and the Four Fires. They chanted as they walked:

'Brigantia, we thank you,
For fire in our hearth at home.
For fire in our working hands.
For fire in our singing souls.
And for fire in our loving hearts.
Binding us together as one.'

As the incantation continued, Edric and Maawan each picked up a stone from the circle, a symbol of the earth, and tossed it into the sea. As they threw the stones, they called to the spirits of the sacred place to meet them in their oath to one another; a promise to always keep the fire of Brigantia alive.

The flames in the torches of the mounted warriors sparked wildly as the wind from the sea caught hold of them. One warrior dismounted, taking his torch to the bonfire heap, which had been built on the edge of the shore. As he lit it, a cheer went up from the gathered crowd and dancing broke out among them.

Even as the sacred fire ascended heavenward, they were not aware that other fires over Brigantia burned with destruction and chaos.

CHAPTER TWELVE

LIGE

Lies

CARTIMANDUA TRAVELLED SOUTH to meet with Roman Principals to seek extra support in the fight against her own people. They promised to send auxiliaries to help subdue Brigante agitators.

'Venutius is building a considerable army of Brigante rebels who are ready to fight against you,' whispered high Druid, Donnlugh, in the ear of the queen.

The queen arrived back at the now partially ruined Isurium, camping there over the winter months. Guarded by a palatinum of Roman warriors, she was able to gain some ground in repairing the buildings in the fort and re-establish a base for her royal company. There, she made plans to oppose the rebellion, something she had to do to keep good accord with her Roman allies.

Her spies were sent out across the land, seeking information about numbers and positions of rebel forces. Donn Donnlugh led the incentive, using his own Druid ability to see beyond reality, into the otherworld. He gleaned knowledge while shapeshifting, viewing vast areas of Brigantia.

'Be warned that Venutius intends to head south toward Mamucium and is probably already there,' Donnlugh advised. 'Meanwhile, the Romans have begun to build a stockade at Deva. Legions are marching toward the west and will halt there until given the word,' he continued, informing the queen of designated troops given to her at the order of the ally Governor, Gallus.

'From these troops, you must order parties of raiders to travel across your lands, listening for anything remotely seditious. Ordering raids on the settlements that bare signs of allegiance with Venutius would be advised.'

'Victory or death!' was her battle cry.

So even as the festival of re-birth approached, when her people would be waiting for light to return to the earth, the queen sent darkness over her lands. Like a Druid cloak, the darkness spread through the east and south, spewing clouds in its wake; the only source of light being from the raging fires as sept after sept was burned. The queen's raiders sped over the hills, through forests, and across rivers in their quest to subdue the rebellion. Home after home, and family after family were tortured, and killed. Some were given the opportunity to realign with Cartimandua an oath of allegiance to Rome, but many did not.

The newly married Lady of Gabrantovices lay at the side of her husband, not daring to think about what she had done, but hoping that she could keep her secret forever.

Their promise to each other was the most real thing she had ever vowed. She meant every word of it. She recalled every minute of her wedding day, savouring the delight of it all. The celebration had gone on until the last candle had died and the moon had disappeared in the light of the morning. Maawan had danced with her lord, had held him, and made love to him until she felt the love inside her body burning with a passion she had never experienced.

She wanted to be with him every moment of her life. Her heart skipped when she thought of him. She touched his hand as he slept at her side. She touched his cheek, and his chest. His young healthy body brought a thrill rippling through every nerve, and she wanted him to take her again.

'Edric, she whispered. 'Edric.'

Edric turned toward her, and without opening his eyes, he leaned into her, smelling her hair, and smiling. 'My wife,' he said, with complete contentment in his voice. He ran his hand down her side as he pulled her closer. 'Shall we join again, my love?' he asked.

Bianna and Dugall had stayed later into the night, as people started moving away from the hilltop and back to their beds. Dugall lay in the circle, enjoying the fragrance from the heavily scented bower over the stone circle.

The fire was still burning, and Bianna sat at Dugall's side, watching the flames flicker. She remembered their wedding night. A smile spread across her lips as she thought about the intimate moment when they became one.

She had wondered occasionally through her young life, about how it might feel to give herself to her husband, but the tenderness and love expressed by Dugall on that first evening had surprised her. She knew the intensity and passion of that experience would stay with her for ever.

As the days unfolded, Bianna began to understand how much Dugall had loved her, even before he asked for her hand. She knew they were meant to be together. Her thoughts meandered as she realised that this loving was special; endorsed by the gods. She prayed that Edric and his bride might also be granted the same eternal blessing.

Dyn was still singing softly outside the circle and poking the fire with his fey. The sea breathed in and out as it lapped the edges of the shore. Clouds parted to reveal the moon, making a pathway across the sea. White and golden steps led from the shore to the heavens.

Bianna stood, startling Dyn. He could see the light of the moon reflected in her eyes and knew that she would follow the path. He followed as she reached the very edge of the hilltop, where she stretched invisible wings and flew toward the white light.

Dugall followed behind her, flying above the clouds, circling round over the sea, and back toward the land. From this vantage point, Dugall could see smoke from the fire, and beyond, more smoke and more fires. Flames lashed at the houses and people below, without mercy.

There was devastation and death all around.

Bianna flew further afield, taking in the holocaust being revealed to her. Flames and ash rose from the ground creating a shield of smoke, stinging Bianna's eyes. In Drueidan, she called for a calming wind to blow the smoke away from her.

Shock overtook her. Sitting in an eagle's nest and vaunting to the moon was a dragon, spewing flames and smoke over Brigantia. The smoke rose to the heavens. Bianna started to choke. She felt herself spiralling upwards into the noxious cloud as it transmuted into the black cloak of Donn; wrapping round her until not a breath remained.

Dugall caught her as she fell and carried her back along the sea path to the hilltop, placing her in the circle. He called to the goddess Brigga to heal her while Dyn wrapped her body in a cloak of warm fur. Together they carried her back to the village.

Dugall had seen enough to know that fire was raging not far from Gabrantovices. Once he had put Bianna in a safe place and made sure she was recovering, he called for the other Druids. The sun was coming up, and although he doubted that Edric would be in a good state, talk to him he must. He first entered the barn where the Roman prisoner had been kept. He flapped his Druid's cloak, swinging it wide in front of the soldier's face until he woke.

Dugall dragged the man up by the rope that held his tattered cape to his shoulders. 'This is your last opportunity to tell us what you know of the queen and the Protectorate. What are their plans?' he asked, as he held the weakened man by the throat. He drew out his dagger and pointed it against his cheek.

'All I know is already told. Lord Edric — I spoke with him,' he said.

'Then you know that you are already dead.'

'No, I beg of you!' Osma had entered the shelter and ran between Dugall and Lucius. 'I implore you. Do not take his life, Dugall.'

Dugall looked at the despairing face of his captive, and then at Osma, as she begged for his life. His mind became a battlefield.

'Where are the gods when you need them?' he thought. 'I should kill him. He deserves it.'

'What will it matter if I spare him?' he asked Osma, who still stood her ground between the two men, as resolute as a Brigante warrior. Deserving or not, Dugall had to admire her spirit, and ceded.

He released the neck cord, and the soldier sank to the ground, gasping for air. Dugall kicked him and walked away.

By evening, Edric joined the forum of Druids and warriors who made up the newly formed council in Gabrantovices. They had been in conference all day. Bianna told the company what she had seen in the vision, and immediately Edric moved to assemble his army to find and strengthen any settlements damaged by the fires. The men were aware of the danger they might be putting themselves in but were compelled to help anyone who sided with Venutius. Edric urged his men to prepare for the journey, packing anything they thought might be of value in their aid. He explained to Maawan that he expected to be away for a few weeks but would return before the festival of Beltane.

'I will ask Camulo and Maccar to stay with both you and Bianna. It will be your assignment to keep the settlement running and keep the women and children safe,' Edric said. Maawan bowed before her lord.

Heaving a sigh of relief, Maawan assured Edric. 'I will send spies out in the next weeks to watch for your return. We will be safe and will prepare for your homecoming,' she said, but her thoughts spoke other things.

'This tumult I have created is pulling me further from my love. What if my position and my lies are uncovered?' she worried. 'I am tangled in deceit while truth must remain hidden.'

The armed men advanced on the road toward Isurium, staying their journey each time, they came upon a village or gathering where the fires had raged. Time was given to assess the damage, help with obsequies and secure where possible against further raids. Cartimandua had caused much damage to her people, and these new assaults only intensified their anger. The more she tried to stop them aligning with Venutius against the Romans, the more their resolve grew in support of him.

It was then that the Braint, headed by Beorand Byrde gathered from all over Brigantium to offer their expertise in the war against the decimation of their people. Great warriors and warriors from small communities alike wanted to join Edric in his plans to march on their mutual enemy in retaliation. The army was growing, but camps of Roman ancillaries were also growing. With brute strength and determination, the Brigante warriors became like savages. They wreaked havoc wherever they found Romans occupying the routes.

As dusk settled, they silently circled one of the auxiliary camps very near to Cawthorn, less than two days ride from home. After waiting for the proper moment, they began their assault. With shouting, carnyx sounding, and waving of swords, they rushed into the camp, beheading as many of the enemy as they could. The opponents were swift to strike back, but the sudden onslaught gave Edric and his men the advantage. The expert horsemen swept through the camp with ease. Three of the Brigante sped toward the Roman horses, releasing them; smacking their backsides till they ran off into the forest beyond.

There was no escape for the enemies, as the mounted warriors galloped round and round the circle, capturing the Triarius within. Legs were sliced and feet were severed in the counterattack; but the wounds were minimal compared to the deaths incurred that day by the Brigante.

The trophy hunting exceeded any past hoard. Dugall offered to travel home with a few men, to take the trophies back.

'I think it would be better if we all travelled back to Gabrantovices, Dugall. The men are tired. The weather is harder. Now we see the damage caused to so many of the villages and settlements. Their defences need to be put in place. We need a co-ordinated plan to help them,' Edric responded. 'Come the spring, we have more chance of impacting. And still, we must join Venutius and help with his plan at Deva.'

Dugall thought and agreed. 'Rest and preparation then. We have but a few weeks.'

'We will rest tonight, and deal with the wounded. But I do not want to lose any more men in skirmishes. I have learned something from my conversations with our captured foe. We can utilise that Latin knowledge a little.'

Yetta approached the door to Bianna's room and knocked on it. She opened the door a little and peeped inside. Bianna was sitting up on the bed with her mother's trinket box open at her side.

She looked up. 'Come in Yetta. I have need to talk to you.'

Yetta wasn't surprised at this, as her mistress seemed to know everything before it happened.

'My lady,' she greeted, as she bobbed her knee. Bianna patted the bed, indicating that she wanted Yetta to sit with her. Obediently, Yetta did as she was bid.

'My lady, I have something to ask.'

'Beored has asked for your hand?' This was more of a statement than a question.

'Is there nothing I can withhold from you?'

'I am delighted, Yetta. He is a good man, and I am sure that Edric will be delighted too.' Yetta beamed with relief. Bianna went on. 'But there is something I must ask you.' She waited till she knew that Yetta's attention was fully focussed on her, and then continued. 'Some time ago, you received into your protection, an item. I spoke of it, telling you that I would require it one day. This is the day, Yetta. I would like you to fetch it and bring it to me.'

Without speaking another word, Yetta rose, leaving the room to fetch the ring she found so long ago. She had wondered often about the significance of the band and had intended to ask Bianna. But time had gone on, and Yetta had almost forgotten about it. She would be glad to give it to her mistress, and glad that Bianna had seen in her all-knowing wisdom that Yetta had not stolen it, but rather had been safekeeping it.

Bianna knew instinctively to whom the ring belonged. All her past visions flooded into her mind with clarity as soon as she saw it. She thanked Yetta for looking after it, before rising to visit Maawan.

Outside, Maawan was tending to the sheep. She looked up as Bianna approached. She smiled, but Bianna did not smile back. Maawan put the pitchfork down and wiped her hands on her skirts.

'What is it, Bianna?' asked Maawan, trying to determine what could be the purpose of this visit.

'Maawan, I am curious about some things, and would like to ask about them,' she said.

'Shall we walk a little, Bianna?' Maawan pointed toward the cairn and began to walk toward it. Sitting overlooking the Great Northern Sea, she prompted Bianna to sit next to her. For a while they sat, taking in the rolling tide and the heavy surf touching the shore beneath them. Maawan knew that this might be the time to be truthful. Holding in the fear of being found out was becoming increasingly difficult when she loved Edric so much.

Maawan began the dialogue. 'Bianna, I want you to know, if you do not know already, that I love Edric with all my heart. We are bound together as one soul. I would give up any birth right to be by his side.'

Bianna responded softly. 'The gods have ordained your union, Maawan, of that, I am sure. But what of your past? When will you tell Edric who you are?'

Maawan fell silent. She wondered how much Bianna knew, and how much she was simply guessing. Either way, she was concerned that her life may well be in jeopardy. Not wanting to risk speaking, Maawan remained silent. The tide throbbed in rhythm with the pounding of her heart.

Bianna revealed the signet ring, pulling it from the folds of her skirt. Maawan put her hand to her mouth, trying to stop crying out. Tears began to fall from her eyes as she realised that indeed, Bianna did know the significance of that ring.

'I am sorry,' she wept. 'I am so sorry.' Bianna nodded, then put her arms around her sister's shoulders as she sobbed. 'What am I to do, Bianna? I want to tell Edric, but I dare not.' The two women sat for a long time, watching the sea birds diving into the cold blue ocean. A cormorant appeared in the sky above them. He settled on the sea by the coastline, bobbing on the water. With one swoop into the cold depths, he disappeared from view. Rising again with precision, the giant bird shook his catch of fish and flew off.

Bianna spoke then. 'The brave and spirited cormorant flies over the water, looking for fulfilment. He waits patiently; suddenly diving deeply. He is hidden from view for a long time, but he catches his desires, and is satisfied. It is the order of the world. And so it is with you, Maawan. The gods have gifted you with a good spirit; one that brings blessings to your people. You dive deeply to catch and keep your heart's desire, but your concealment cannot last for ever. You must resurface from your hiding place and allow the gods to weave their schemes.'

She handed the ring to Maawan, rose from the grass, and bowed as she walked away.

Several weeks passed before Edric and his growing army returned to Gabrantovices. A scout had travelled before them, to give word of their approach. As is the way of the Brigante people, feasts were prepared, and the homecoming was anticipated with excitement. Some of the additional warriors went on the way back to wife and family, but many did not, and the sept was soon teeming with new faces. There numbered about sixty, including a few women warriors. Make-shift shelters were erected as bed space. Hunting parties were arranged, and before long stags and boars found their way to the spits around the centre circle of the sept.

Days were spent getting to know the new arrivals, ranking their abilities, and positioning them in the new Gabrantovices army. Edric, already *Beornraed* in Gabrantovices, had been elevated to 'Lord Chief' in the hearts of the Tyro allies too. He was aware that arrogance so often causes men to trip and look foolish, so he guarded his heart from pride. Even so, his confidence grew with each day, as he saw the expertise of his warriors strengthen.

Emissaries of Venutius carried news to all rebel leaders across Brigantia, asking for their aid in the fight against invasion. They arrived at Gabrantovices and brought the report to Edric, and the council. 'Venutius and his army are gathering strength. He knows of the Roman's intent to take the island of Ynys Môn so they can destroy the Druidic training base, once and for all. A number of men are already on their way to Mamucium, as Venutius planned. They will build a stronghold there, then send men in all directions, but especially to Deva to destroy the Roman fort being erected there.' the messengers relayed. 'Venutius hopes that this will delay the Roman legions heading toward Ynys Môn.'

Edric confirmed, 'Tell Venutius, we are already preparing and will join with him and our brother Brigante in the fight against these tyrants.'

❦

The sun was beginning to warm the earth. The planting had gone well; a good harvest for that year was foretold. By the end of spring the plans were in place for the army's departure, venturing toward Mamucium to join Venutius.

Edric and Maawan walked to the top of the cairn. They looked out to sea, taking in the soul music that played each time their spirits allowed. They held hands. This was the day of parting, the night before the great withdrawal to meet Venutius and battle against the enemy.

This was the day that Maawan had chosen to tell Edric of her heritage.

As she stood by Eric's side, Maawan began to shake. Edric noticed her trembling. He took his cloak from his shoulders and placed it on the ground. He prompted her to sit by his side. Her nearness brought tingles to his body. Wrapping his arms around her, he held her tight, transferring his body heat. They sat together for some time; Maawan internally preparing to speak the truth.

"I will tell him now. Where is my courage?' she wondered. Edric held her close, kissing her hair, her head, and neck. He leaned forward, lifting her face to meet his, gently tracing her mouth with his lips. His body filled with passion, as Maawan moved to meet him in the kiss.

Edric whispered, 'I need you, princess. I need you,' and softly he laid her down onto the cloak. He wrapped the folds round the two of them, as they joined together in love.

They lay side by side, listening to the tide breathing in and out as it kissed the shore. 'I want the world to stop,' Maawan whispered. 'Make this moment last forever,' she said. Edric lay silently, feeling the rhythm of the tide match his own breathing, he thought of the depth of his desire for his wife. He never expected to feel this level of intensity. 'This is so good,' he thought.

Maawan touched Edric's hand. 'Edric,' she said softly, daring to risk her confession. 'Edric, I love you so very much. The gods have put us together, I am sure,' she began. 'But I have something I need to tell you, and it breaks my heart that you will not receive it.' Edric did not respond at first, as his thoughts were still enjoying the flavour of Maawan's body.

'Edric, I lied to you.'

This news filtered leisurely through his sweet thoughts, but as his mind began to grasp the statement, he rolled over to face Maawan.

'What lie?'

Maawan offered the signet ring of Cartimandua to Edric. As Maawan began to tell Edric the truth about her birth, Edric rose, moving away from her. He turned toward the sea, with his back to her, and let the truth sink in. Maawan began to plead with him, telling him that she had already given up any birth right as the heir to Brigantia, and, she explained, '*You*, my love, mean so much more than the whole of Brigantia. I will gladly fight with you against my mother…'

'Silence!' shouted Edric. He turned to look at the crying heap in front of him, and anger flared in his chest. 'You lied! You have put me in an indefensible position. You cannot fight with Venutius. He wants to kill you. He wants the throne for himself — and will have it! He will not risk his victory by allowing you to live.' Edric began to pace backwards and forwards as the full extent of this revelation became clearer. 'You are my enemy. My sworn enemy! Are you the traitor among us?'

Maawan cried, 'No, my lord. I have only ever loved you. From the moment you killed Taexalin, I have loved you. I am not your enemy.' She crawled toward him, grabbing his leg as she pleaded.

Kicking himself free of her grasp, he seized hold of Maawan, pulling her frightened face close to his. At that moment, he didn't know whether to kill her, such was his turmoil. He threw her to one side and walked away. Maawan sank to the ground.

Great sobs of utter humiliation welled from her eyes until her vision blurred. Among the sobs, she whispered to Edric, and to the gods. 'I am with child, Edric. I am with child.' Her voice was lost in the wind.

CHAPTER THIRTEEN

Saorsa
Liberty

BEFORE HE LEFT, Dugall arranged for Bianna to meet him at Ynys Môn; she was to make her way there as soon as she heard of victory against the Romans at Deva.

'We will look for a new life for a while, Bianna; one where we can raise children in safety, where we can help our brothers and sisters keeping the faith. But we must be careful. It is a dangerous route, but the only one we have, if we are to help our fellow Druids. One day we will return to Gabrantovices, but for a while, until the chaos stops, we will settle there, if the gods allow.'

'I have seen it in the visions, Dugall. I know what lies ahead is dangerous. But the gods would not have given revelation, unless what is seen, is also part of the solution. I will meet you there,' she responded, nodding in agreement, and making to leave. Then turning back toward Dugall, she asked, 'Dugall, do you think there is any hope for our priests and our ancient ways?'

'I hope so, Bianna. I hope so.' But Dugall's countenance was sombre and his mouth drooped downwards. 'I know a refuge; a safe place we can head toward.' Dugall gave Bianna the details. She repeated the instructions over, until she remembered them in her heart. Lifting her into his arms, he kissed her.

Edric went to his bedroom, and from his mother's box he removed the 'birth right' document. The ancient runes lay before him in Ogham. He could see the symbol of Taranis, his father's chosen emblem, and the token of the High Druid, Donn Donnlugh. Other runes and lines were set down the parchment, but Edric could not understand their meaning. He stuffed the scroll into his tunic, promising himself he would find Dugall at the earliest opportunity, and ask him to decipher it.

The warriors from Gabrantovices set their sights toward Mancunium. The army convoy numbered more than two hundred, including infantry and workers walking at the side of the battle horses and cart ponies. Edric held the lead position, flanked by Beored and Buite. Dugall followed, carrying the flag of Brigantia and the sign of Venutius.

Bianna and Camulo stayed behind with the intent of making their way to Ellestob, along with Maawan and Dyn. The settlement was left, once again, in the overall authority of Maccar and Cerdic.

Edric did not look back as he rode through the gate. His anger toward Maawan still seethed. He had neither looked at her nor spoken a word to her since her confession. His only conversation was to ask Camulo to keep her safe.

Under cover of night, Bianna, Camulo, Dyn, and Maawan left the sept. The road was more dangerous, now that Cartimandua had escalated her quest to subdue her people. Mercenaries, rebels, and bandits littered the pathways. The Romans were infiltrating every part of Brigantia. Bianna threw a Druid cloak of invisibility across the four of them, which helped, but did not completely hide them. Camulo was on constant guard.

They travelled as swiftly as the horses would take them, resting only for periods when cloud covered the moon, making it impossible to venture further. As the moon disappeared into the blackness, Camulo dismounted. Quietly, they found a concealed clearing by a thicket. They crawled through the bushes and trees, and into the shrouded spot. It was sufficiently hidden for Maawan and Bianna to feel safe enough to settle into sleep for a while.

Camulo and Dyn kept watch. An owl hooted as it swooped after his prey. A stag silently passed. A twig snapped. Camulo, already on his feet and with sword drawn, peered through the darkness for the source of the noise.

In a flash of bronze, an arrow passed through Camulo's shoulder. He dropped the sword, crying out. Bianna jumped up and went for the horses. Calling to Maawan, she instructed her to mount and flee. 'I will follow,' she shouted. Running to Camulo in the darkness, Dyn helped him onto his horse, and swiftly mounting their own horses, the four were away.

Galloping behind Maawan, the black rider bolted to catch

her. Maawan rode her horse as never before. An arrow sped toward her, catching the side of the horse. Maawan called to the gods for help. She stirred up the wounded horse, calling his name and encouraging him to continue.

'Come on, my lovely,' she whispered, her head low on the neck of the beast. He responded, his hooves beating a four-gait gallop. His nostrils flared, taking in as much air as possible. The moon appeared from behind the clouds, enough for Maawan to see a little farther along the path. She could hear Bianna shouting behind her. She continued to gallop, without knowing where her enemy rode. Suddenly the horse faltered, catching his leg in brambles. Maawan fell from the horse, as another arrow whizzed above her head.

The black horse was upon her before she could stand. The rider grabbed her arm, lifting her easily onto the back of his horse, and galloped away.

Bianna, Dyn, and the wounded Camulo searched for their lady even as the moon faded into dawn. She had disappeared, with only her horse to be found. Urgently returning to Ellestob, Camulo (though wounded) sent two messengers: one to Edric and one to Gabrantovices, asking them to be on alert, should the kidnapper take Maawan back there. He ordered a contingent of scouts and warriors to follow the trail that the black rider took

'The lady must be found!' he warned.

As soon as Edric received the news of the Maawan's disappearance, he ordered his men to continue marching toward Mamucium.

'I will respond to Camulo. I leave now. Wulfnud and Gedrae will accompany me. I will return as soon as Maawan is found.' Fear gripped his heart. Why should he be concerned about Maawan? She was a liar and a cheat. His heart sickened even at the thought of her. He loved her but hated her. He sped off with the two others, not knowing how he would react when he found her. They took the east path facing Gabrantovices, till it divided to join the northern road on the west of Isurium. After two hot days of riding, they arrived at where Maawan had been taken.

The Ellestob scouts had picked up a trail from the galloping horse and could point Edric in the direction the rider had gone. The four warriors from Ellestob had already begun to follow the tracks. When Edric and the others caught up, the men had silently surrounded the camp of the black-cloaked kidnapper.

Maawan was tied round the waist to a tree; her mouth gagged.

The man sat on a log to her left; his face hidden by his hood. All the while, he turned a skewered rabbit over a small fire, picking at his kill with his dagger.

'You see, little lady, I know who you are. Your head will make me rich,' he said, spitting out some skin from the meat as he pulled it with his teeth. 'Edric will give me good money to save you, so we will wait a while for him to appear.'

Edric took in the situation as he approached. Should the captor throw the knife, Maawan would be harmed, or worse. But he realised that the woman-snatcher likely would not do that, if there was any chance of a bargain on her life. Edric moved toward the camp, signalling to his men to stay where they were. The surrounding warriors watched in readiness.

As Edric approached the fire, a voice came from beneath the hood. 'Hello Edric, old friend,' he said as Edric moved nearer. 'I wondered how long you might be.' He did not lift his head to look up as Edric approached. Edric scanned the side of the bandit, noticing the double lining of his black cloak. Green folds showed under the hood.

The circling warriors moved into positions where they could be seen by the cloaked man. They surrounded the camp, making it clear that there was no escape for the abductor. Even so, he casually took another bite at the spiked meat, before turning to front Edric.

Revealed beneath the folds of the dark covering, sat his old scout, Tiernan. A scar ran from the side of his cheek up to his disfigured ear; the top of which was missing. Tiernan watched Edric, as he noticed the scar.

'Take a good look at the damage you inflicted,' he said, as he pulled the hood away from his head. 'I was in pain, losing blood and you did not come to help me,' he moaned. 'Ediva was distraught, yet you still did not care.' A glint of hatred flashed from his narrowed eyes, as he raised his dagger in front of Maawan. 'But do not fret, Edric Bloodeworthe, for your retribution is not far away. Maybe a slice off your woman's ear will take away some of my pain.'

Tiernan leaned forward as if to cut Maawan's ear, then taking the threat away, he laughed. Edric remained silent, as he made to sit by Maawan.

'Ha-ha! How the god's have retooled our lives, Edric Bloodeworthe,' Tiernan laughed, sneering at Edric. 'I have sent word to Cartimandua that I hold her daughter. She rides this way, presently.'

Edric shook his head in disbelief. 'The queen is too busy to listen to a messenger sent by you. Why would she even think of it? I doubt she has even heard your name.'

'She will listen, because Ediva brought the message supported by

Romans in Parisii. They, at least, hold me in great respect,' shouted Tiernan in a rage. Edric smiled while keeping a close eye on the knife being held so close to Maawan's face as Tiernan twisted it round and round. 'My reputation in Parisii is not a small one.'

Tiernan's fury eased, and he took another bite of the meat. Bolus spit out of his mouth as he spoke, 'I have also told our goddess queen who it is that has been holding her daughter all this time, and of your violation of her precious child.'

Edric silently weighed this information. He needed to get Maawan away, quickly, before the place was covered with Roman soldiers. He tensed at the thought. Catching the furtive look that Edric shot round the camp, Tiernan continued, 'Are you in a hurry, Bloodeworthe? I have all the time I need. The queen will be here soon enough,' he sniggered. 'I have a question for you. When Venutius realises that his ally has married the next heir to Brigantia, how do you think he will feel about your loyalty, Edric?'

Appearing as relaxed as he could, Edric sat at the other side of Maawan, and faced Tiernan. In silence, he waited for the pompous man to continue.

'I am no longer Tiernan the Timid! I am The Green Cloak of Darkness, Donn Gearr!' His chest expanded with pride as he introduced his new self. 'But I have never forgiven you, Edric Bloodeworthe, for the way you mistreated me, and for leaving my sister out of your life. She loved you. But *you*, in your arrogance, instead took the daughter of our queen and bedded her!' Teirnan spat into the fire and twisted the knife in his hand. 'We will wait. Our queen will be here before the sun rises. And I will be standing at her side when she beheads you.'

Edric moved slowly to take Maawan's hand, trying to comfort her.

It was true that he could give the word and the warriors would swoop to their defence, but Teirnan needed to be distracted before Edric could take that risk.

Silently he prayed to the gods, and to the gods of the Romans, for good measure.

Bianna knelt at the shrine of Ogbrig; the god bringing light and understanding to the heart of his people. She sought knowledge of the whereabouts of her sister-in-law, and insight into how she might intervene to bring her back to Ellestob. She had taken *couchen* mixed with dried mushrooms that morning; a Druid drink that worked powerfully on the mind. She chanted, swaying back and forth as she invoked the god's help. She slipped backward in a *dwam,* falling to the ground as Ogbrig appeared before her; his large and formidable self, towering over her.

No words sounded between them. Bianna's eyes, fully open, showed dilated pupils. She moved her head from side to side as her lips mouthed shapes of words which were not uttered. Ogbrig looked deep into her eyes, allowing a shaft of light from his to Bianna's; she, absorbing the power he transferred. He gifted her knowledge, as she shape-shifted to become a jackdaw. Ogbrig showed her where Maawan was being held, and she flew westward.

As she approached the camp, she settled on the tree, a branch above Maawan. With a keen eye, Bianna watched from above as the scene played out below. Edric had taken Maawan's hand to comfort her, Bianna assumed. She flew silently to the back of the tree, pecking round about the base of the trunk. With a step here, and a hop there, she closed in on the rope tied tightly round Maawan's body. She picked at the rope until she felt it slacken.

Carefully Maawan fidgeted the rope away. When Edric took her hand, she squeezed it.

'I am free,' she thought, hoping somehow, he would understand.

Bianna flew back into the tree. From that lofty position, Bianna was able to see the glint of the blade, ready to be propelled from Tiernan's hand, in the direction of Maawan.

With one great swoop, Bianna landed on Tiernan's head; cackling loudly in his ear to disorientate him. He knocked her away, but she flew for his eyes, clawing at them. She fought for the dagger, pecking at his fist until she drew blood. The dagger dropped from his hand as he went to brush the blood from his eyes. In that split second, Edric was on his feet. He swung Maawan away from the tree, sprinting with her to the outskirts of the camp. He signalled the warriors, and they marched on the hooded enemy, tearing him from limb to limb.

Maawan clung to Edric, sobbing into his warm tunic, as he released the gag from around her mouth. He tightened his grip round her, feeling the closeness between them. He wanted to hold her, comfort her: wondering if forgiveness had settled in his heart. But still, the threat of death hung over her shoulder and took over his senses. He signalled to Gedrae to bring horses.

'Get Maawan back to Ellestob, Gedrae. Take her to safety.' He turned to Maawan. 'Go and wait for my return. I need to lead my men as we planned, but I will return. Go to Ellestob. You will be safe with Camulo and Dyn. Wait for me there.' As an afterthought, he turned to Gedrae again, and added, 'If I am not back within six days of

Imbolc, take Maawan to Gabrantovices. I will be there as soon as I can.'

Maawan leaned closer into Edric. She pulled him urgently toward her, whispering in his ear. She asked for his forgiveness and told him of the child she was expecting.

'The child should be with us by Imbolc,' she explained. This news shocked him. He wanted to hold Maawan; to tell her that everything would be alright.

He wanted to add, 'And I love you and forgive you,' but the words stuck in his throat, and he could not. She kissed him, and then with one easy action, Maawan was on the back of the horse following swiftly behind Gedrae as he led the warriors and scouts toward home.

Bianna, now returned from the shape shifting, stood by the remains of the Gabrantovices turncoat, and wept for the death, guilt, and betrayal that this civil war had reaped upon her own. From deep within her being, she felt the pain of war and loss. A silent scream welled up in her mind. Her tears flowed. Edric returned and called her to sit by his side a little way from the blood and entrails.

'Are you harmed?' he asked. Bianna did not respond to this question.

'Help me move the body into the woods. The gods of the forest will take him home.' She was weary, and grateful that Edric was there. Edric told her of his news, that he would be a father before the spring was over.

'The news has shocked me, Bianna. I did think I might become a father one day, but I hadn't thought about it until now. I don't know how I feel about it. I know it's a great responsibility. I don't know if I am ready for such a sacred burden; nor whether I am ready to forgive Maawan for deceiving me as she has.'

'Edric, I have a propensity for believing that the gods are weaving their plans, and all will work out accordingly,'

'Then take care of her, Bianna. I am still fearful for her safety. Who knows how Cartimandua will take this news…?'

Bianna nodded. 'I had a vision, Edric. The baby must be born in Gabrantovices. It is the will of our gods. There is a ritual which must be completed at the birth. It will carry the blessing of Brigantia.' She took Tiernan's horse and left, riding to Ellestob.

Edric mounted his own black steed and with Wulfnud at his side, they hastened back to meet their army of marching warriors. Heading southwest, they rode the farm paths and narrow lanes, hoping to avoid a collision with Cartimandua. Realising that she would probably be travelling with a small army, they knew the chance of the two of them being able to take her was unlikely. They rested for two nights before continuing toward Mamucium.

They saw the Brigante camps as they approached: the mass covered the hillside from north to south. Each tribe had planted its colours in the centre of their camp circle, so it was easy for Edric to find his men among the hundreds of war bases. The riders were quick to join their men and exchange news of the campaign and the whereabouts of Cartimandua.

Cartimandua, meanwhile, travelled with Donn Donnlugh, the High Druid, and a contingency of heavily armed Roman soldiers to the location identified by her scouts. She travelled in a wooden chariot, with two attendants and Ediva. Donnlugh and the soldiers followed on horseback. She dismounted and took in the scene. The green-cloaked corpse had already been gorged by Veridois; the god who returns everything to the earth. Cartimandua was not accustomed to her desires being dashed. She clenched her jaw, then spitting in anger and frustration, she called Ediva to her side.

'You will go with your brother!' she screamed, and with one swipe from her long sword, she liberated Ediva's head from her shoulders. Anger boiled inside the royal heart.

Wherever her daughter was, whether dead or alive, Cartimandua wanted to know.

'Find this treacherous son of a whore who has taken my daughter,' she roared. 'He will hang from the nearest tree till wild animal's feast on his heart, and I, personally will cut off his defiance and roast it!' She ordered three warriors to scout the area for any clues to the whereabouts of the princess and sent three warriors to find a place to stay before they journeyed back to Isurium, to war. Donnlugh proposed he personally make a fresh search for Maawan before he returned to the queen at Isurium.

'I will venture toward Gabrantovices, and search there,' he offered, as he raked through the remains of Donn Gearr to read any bones that may give insight.

'But I will look for her later,' he thought. 'First, I have other things to settle with Edric Beorand, Lord Bloodeworthe…' Donn Donnlugh silently trailed Edric and Wulfnud, keeping far enough behind to allow himself cover.

At night he hovered nearer to Edric's camp, watching, and waiting.

CHAPTER FOURTEEN

DONN DONNLUGH
The Dark One

BOREUS AND HIS GROUP of ten, sent to stop the Roman army from marching through to Mancunium, went to ground at Wyndgate Pass. On their way to the Pass, they collected other supporters and weaponry. There they waited to ambush the enemy troops. They hid high up on each side of the limestone ridges: from this lofty vantage point, they were able to see the Centuria as it snaked up the steep path cut deeply between the mountainous walls.

The Romans would be easy targets for Boreus' men who positioned themselves in a human line running along the top of both sides of the ravine. Those occupying the highest elevations, where to start shooting arrows and throwing spears as soon as the enemy neared the top of the Pass. Then, working down the line, they were to continue until the bottom shooters joined in. A simple plan, but with the element of surprise on the Brigante side. They were to continue for as long as they had munitions, or until the entire Roman troop were finished.

Waiting for the front riders and infantry to reach the top of the pass, Boreus gave the order:

'Sound the Carnyx! In the name of freedom and Brigantium!'

Arrows and spears pelted down into the marching procession. Dead men and horses fell, causing a block at the exit of the pass. As riders tried to turn round and find escape from the torrent of metal beating down on them, they were met with another blasting from the entrance of the pass. Confusion and panic took hold as soldiers tried to circle for a place of safety. Some tried riding up the wall of the mountain, but the wet grass and stones saw most of them slip and flip backwards onto the piling bodies of the dead. Some, as they turned to escape, trampled on confrere — and still the arrows flew.

The Brigante warriors shot continuously, until their arrows were depleted, and the last of the spears had landed. Few riders escaped that day.

Back in Vincobancia, the men praised Edric's shrewd planning and Boreus' leadership. They praised their warrior's skill, lifting their tankards and shouting, 'Brigantia!,' 'Brigantia and Taranis!'

'Sleep well, brave men. Tomorrow our journey continues. Tomorrow, we progress toward Mamucium to meet our fellow sword rattlers! Our war is not over yet!' Boreus shouted above the clamour of drunken noise.

The messenger sent by Camulo arrived back at the sept in Gabrantovices and went straight to Cerdic. He explained the circumstances of Maawan's birth, and the danger that she was in. Cerdic immediately wanted to send further support to Ellestob. He knew they would be safe in the Hidden Isle, but he would make plans to transfer the princess and her guards back to Gabrantovices in time for Edric's return and Imbolc, as planned.

Bianna had insisted on the return, explaining, 'Cerridwen, the giver of wisdom, came to me in a vision. She spoke of pain and trauma, of threat and death, but also about a birth, a significant omen. When the new moon collides with Imbolc, the birth of caul and fire must be washed in fresh sea water.' Such was Bianna's insistence, that the plan to return to Gabrantovices was executed, despite the danger.

Cerdic enquired after Camulo's health.

'He is quite well and will soon return to his former strength. Two more entire moon cycles, and he will have reached his battle brawn again,' reported the messenger.

'This is good to know. Then I will send help until Camulo is back to full fitness. We will have an assembly together by tomorrow at noon. Travel back with them and give Camulo and his people our salutations.' At this, Cerdic left to find Maccar and the council of Druids.

Cerdic spoke of the message and circumstances of Maawan's escape from Donn Green Cloak. Maccar volunteered to travel to Ellestob.

'Then go guised as a pilgrim. This will give you a cover for travel,' Cerdic propounded.

'I have a suggestion, Cerdic,' Maccar proposed, stroking his long beard. 'As we must travel near to where the queen is heading, I suggest we might take the captive Roman, Lucius Manus. He could be useful to us. If he is with us, it may seem we have legitimate cause to travel. If we come upon Venutius men, we can use the Roman as a bargaining tool. Either way, it might serve our purpose and allow us to travel more swiftly.'

Cerdic thought on this. 'Then he must be fettered under his cloak, so that it appears either way: he could be free, or he could be a prisoner. What he must not do, is escape and warn our enemies where the princess is,' warned Cerdic. 'Bring them home safely as soon as you can travel with Camulo.'

Maccar left to prepare his horses and baggage and find the messenger, then to the hovel where the Roman remained captive. He entered the foul-smelling prison and dragged the Roman out into the fresh air.

'Bring him water and clean clothes, Osma,' he ordered. Osma had been attending to Lucius every day. His hand had healed well, and although he could no longer hold a sword, Osma had cared for his wounds very well. Maccar did not tell him the plan, but as Osma returned with fresh tunic and bracae, he told him to prepare for a journey. Osma moved to one side, away from the captive.

'Lord Maccar,' she began. 'Lord Maccar, I understand this man, having spent so much time tending to his needs these last months.' She waited for some sign that Maccar was listening to her before she continued. 'I have spoken with him on many subjects and may be able to help you. Is it possible for me to journey with you?' she dared to ask.

Maccar decided that Osma may well be an asset to the comforts of the journey, so without much thought he agreed that she may travel with them.

'Be ready to leave by noon tomorrow,' he said.

Osma could not understand the flutter she felt in her breast at that moment; whether it was excitement for the adventure tomorrow, or that for the first time, she would see her captive in the real light of day. 'What are these feelings I have for this man?' she asked herself, as she helped him wash. 'When I look at him, I feel hot. His closeness makes my skin tingle.'

That evening, as she sat with Lucius, he asked, 'May I speak plainly, my lady?' As she nodded, and looked intently in his eyes, he continued. 'My heart burns with a strong passion. When you are near me, my heart pounds. I cannot think of anything else, except seeing you. Though my desire to be with you seems impossible, do you think there might be a way for love to flourish?'

In response, Osma gave herself to Lucius tentatively, but wholeheartedly.

The journey ensued without interruption. Osma sat and ate with her prisoner, and they talked often, each sharing their religious tenets and differing ways of life, but with furtive touching and hand holding.

Camulo greeted the six as they arrived at the water bridge into Ellestob. 'Come, and welcome,' he smiled. He pointed the two guards to their shelters and beckoned the others toward his hall. Bianna was pleased to see Osma and Maccar. She took Maccar to one side, seeking understanding for the Roman riding with them. Maccar explained the reasoning behind the plan, but also what he had observed during their mission.

'I do believe that Osma is warm toward Lucius, and he toward her. I think Lucius would make a good guard for Maawan, and she will be delighted to receive Osma as her waiting maid, if you agree.' Because Maccar had the wisdom of the old ones, Bianna trusted that that his judgement was sound.

'There is sense in having Lucius as a slave to Maawan,' Bianna thought. 'He would be loyal to her if he knew who she was, of that I have no doubt.'

'Then we will all stay here as Edric requires, Maccar. We will plan our journey back to Gabrantovices after Yule. The Lady Maawan is with child. We must be vigilant for her safety,' Bianna agreed, feeling the wild wind in her hair and understood the god's approval of the plan.

Bianna was delighted to see Osma looking so well. 'Osma, I am pleased you are here. And what of the Roman? Is he to be trusted?' she asked.

'I trust him, my lady. I have found him to be honest and kind.' Her face coloured is she spoke.

'Why, Osma. Is that a look of telling!' she teased. "I do believe you have a liking for this soldier.'

'Bianna, I am in love. We hope to be together. Is there any chance we could be together?' Osma pleaded.

Bianna smiled. 'In good time, Osma. I believe you could. But for now, you must go to Maawan and help her in whatever way she requires. She is our lady and must be treated as such.'

Osma was satisfied, and happy.

When Osma had realised that she too was pregnant, she couldn't wait to tell Maawan. But Lucius must know first.

'How much do you love me, Lucius Manus?' she asked one bright morning. They sat by the river, netting grayling The Lady of the Stream and dangling their feet in the shallow waters edge on the north side of the sept.

Lucius loved his new position as protector of the queen's daughter. He loved Osma too and looked forward to the day when he might have Osma by his side, a home, and children.

'I love you very much, Osma. You know I do.'

'Good,' she responded. 'Then you need to know that I carry our child.' Lucius was overjoyed, and overprotective. Osma loved every minute of his attention.

Maawan was also overjoyed to hear the news. 'When will your child be born, Osma,' she asked.

'Toward the end of Spring, I think,' answered a jubilant Osma.

'And mine, around Imbolc. Just a few weeks earlier.' Maawan calculated. The two women planned the birthing, chattered about babies, and laughed with happiness at the prospect before them.

Lucius guarded the two; his love, Osma, and his lady, Maawan.

Edric looked over his shoulder often. Sometimes he thought he saw a fleeting shadow; sometimes nothing. But a sense of unease rode with him, an unease he recognised from his childhood, and one that seemed to follow him wherever he went.

As the riders approached Mamucium, Donnlugh saw the sprawl of support for Venutius; even more than he had supposed.

'Venutius had gathered enough of an army to defeat Cartimandua, though I doubt the Roman invading army will be touched,' he thought. He and Cartimandua had been warned by Roman governor Gaius Paulinus that twenty thousand men were ready to move north, should they be needed. Though worse than this, he warned that they were ready to take Brigantia, if Cartimandua could not subdue the uprising against her. Donnlugh, realising his time in power as High Druid and judge of Brigantia may well be coming to an end, had the notion that now was the time to take a new life, and fast. 'I have waited many years to collect what is rightfully mine. I have watched on the side-lines too long. I will wait no longer.' he vowed.

Edric was glad to get back to his men, enjoying the camaraderie and battle fever intoxicating the warriors. Talk of strategy to stop the Roman invasion of Deva kept his mind active. There was no space for thoughts of Maawan, Cartimandua, or of self-doubt.

Edric applied all his energy to the task at hand.

Venutius sent out envoys to each camp, explaining his plan for defence of the town, and his plan to stop the Romans from continuing westward toward the Holy Isle of Ynys Môn. The rain had held off for some days now, and rather than wait any longer, Venutius wanted to use the clement weather to surprise the Romans with an early attack.

The Gabrantovice barbarians bared their chests and more, daubing woad symbols on bodies and faces. In a ritual to Epona, The Horse Goddess, they whitened their hair with lime water till it hardened and stood high on their heads. The 'Horse Spirits' were called upon for blessings and protection. They vowed to the gods; their lives in exchange for victory over the Brigante violators. They vowed slaughter, until their land was free once more. As the drums beat out the war cry, their voices rose in insults and sluagh-ghairm.

Edric rallied his men, encouraging them with victory talk as his fighting-spirit soared.

Dugall also encouraged them and spoke of their place in this world and the Otherworld, yet to be experienced.

'Dying is not something to be feared, my brothers, but to be embraced!'

The men understood the Ancient Way, when two worlds meet and mix. They were willing to give their lives in this world, for a new life beyond, should the gods decree. Morale was high, and the men were ready. As they sat together the eve before battle, they ate and drank, enjoying the feast before them. The cold of mid-winter did not seem to penetrate the driving energy of the men. They were cocksure and ready.

As the warriors drank, the bards began to sing; the words floating in the night sky.

The ancient ones recall it still.
The place where worlds collide.
Where winter meets the summer sun;
Where dawn and dusk reside.
And on my journey to this place
I need the oracle

Tina Zee

To enter into 'Otherworld
Through doors unnatural.
Then from my chaos into rest
Leave behind the old
And with that step discover then
The truth the ancients told.'

Dugall sat watching the sky for omens. He noticed a dark cloud hovered over Edric. He watched discreetly as it grew and dominated the sky above them. As he ate, heaviness crept over him. 'Edric, beware this battle,' he said. Edric nodded as if he had also seen and understood the omen.

'Dugall, should anything happen to me, I ask that you protect Maawan and Bianna. I know I have no need to press, but I want to hear you say it.'

'Indeed, Lord Beorand. You have no need to ask. I will, should the need arise. But may Taranis give the power for your life to continue.'

Pulling out the document of birth right, Edric passed it to Dugall. 'Can you tell me what this says, Dugall? It's in the ancient Oak letters and symbols.'

Dugall looked at the symbols drawn on the animal skin scroll. He was quiet for a time. Then looking at Edric, he said, 'Did you know that your father, Edwin Bloodeworthe and Donn Donnlugh were brothers?' He watched Edric's face for any sign of knowledge.

Edric was shocked. 'No. I never knew. What does this mean, Dugall?'

A heavy drop of rain splashed onto the scroll. Then another, and before there was time to hide from the heavens, the deluge hit. The men ran for cover, dropping the scroll in the instant. Lightning flashed, forking onto the tent, and into the ground all around them. Edric watched as the sky lit up with each jagged streak. He watched as the drawings on the scroll disappeared in the flood. The rain stopped as quickly as it had started. A westerly wind blew until there was no sign of water, except for where it should be.

Eric sat quietly as Dugall unfolded a tale. 'When I was going through my apprenticeship to earn my position as warrior Druid, I spent much time on Ynys Môn. There, we learned about the ancient ways: the earth, the sun, the stars, and their passageways from our world into the underworld.

'I visited the place in between our worlds many times. I saw darkness, and I saw light. The two paths are very different; one path is a hard one to travel and return from.' Dugall stroked his chin as if deciding whether to continue. 'Edric, once, I was on the way through the boggy forest. Passing wraith shadows and green fairie glow, I saw a shadow before me. No light could penetrate its darkness. It was as thick as an oak tree. That shadow spoke to me in Drueidan. His name was Donnlugh; Father of darkness and death.'

Edric gasped as Dugall spoke. 'Is this the dark Donn, the High Druid over Brigantia?'

'I believe this is so. This *Llugh* — the one I met in the Otherworld; he spoke about the time to come. He told me of fires over Brigantia, burning everything in its wake. This chaos, he prophesied, would continue for a time, until the eagle flew over the land, quenching the flames. I asked him who he was, and how he knew these things. He said he was Lord of the East, but his lands had been snatched from him. He promised to avenge the thief who took his lands and birth rite. Then I found myself back in this world.'

'What do you think this means Dugall?' asked Edric.

Dugall gazed into the fire. 'This is my understanding of the scroll; it is clear that Donnlugh is your uncle, the eldest of two brothers. I think there is every possibility that your father took the land of Gabrantovices from him.' Edric began to object, but Dugall spoke, holding his hand up to stop the protests. 'Rightly or wrongly, I think Donnlugh wants Gabrantovices and will try and get it by any means he can. There is a possibility that he may try to kill you, Edric, and claim his right for the east.'

Edric remembered his mother's words, as she lay dying on her bed. 'Did she want me to go to Donn Donnlugh and make right a wrong?' he wondered.

As questions swirled round in his head, Dugall continued, this time in a deeper trance.

'As winter meets the summer and two worlds touch, the Exalted One will rise from fire. Through the deep water, *breo-saighead* will carry the Brigante fire which cannot be extinguished. Through this world of chaos, and into the next, the power and strength which is Brigantia will live on as the eternal flame.'

Venutius' army advanced, meeting the Roman army at Deva. They routed the Roman soldiers easily. The surprise worked in Brigante favour. Naked Brigante savages came flooding, shouting, and yelling with bloodthirsty ardour; barbarism and brawn swinging swords and weapons, galloping toward the Roman enemy. Many of the Romans, turned from the scene and fled in blind panic.

The Brigante moved in to take Deva, primarily demolishing the beginnings of the new wooden fort.

They slaughtered any that stood in their way.

In the centre of the battlefront, Venutius called out his orders. Edric and his men drove their horses into the midst of the struggle, swords wielding round as they gathered strength to slice through the throats of any Romans that stayed in defiance. Without a pause, they cleaved through the fray until they had opened a pathway for the men without steed, to run toward the fallen enemy. Axes and hatchets chopped till a runnel of blood filled the field.

With a victory song in their hearts, the warriors camped that night in the ruins of the wooden fort. The Romans had legions of soldiers, who could and would be deployed as soon as possible. He knew General Paulinus would not stop until he had subdued Brigantia. But for that night, Venutius joined with his men, enjoying the triumph.

Edric sat with his men, once again singing, and praising the tactics of the victory. Turning to Dugall, he said, 'Tomorrow I ride to find Donnlugh, this High Priest.'

Dugall replied, 'Take care, Edric. I have a feeling he will find you.'

As the dawn broke through the morning, Edric bade farewell to Dugall and his men. Dugall asked for permission to journey on toward Ynys Môn, and support the Druids there, until the enemy had been vanquished. Edric agreed, with warnings about wisdom and stupidity being two sides of a man's purse. He gave instructions for them to follow him home in time to celebrate Imbolc.

It was less than five days away, and Edric was anxious to get home to tell Maawan he loved her, and that she was all that mattered to him. He was ready to give Donn Donnlugh the lands he held, in return for a safe living for him and his family.

They went their separate ways as Venutius gave orders to his men to travel the breadth and length of Brigantia, ridding the land of any of the queen's men.

Donn Donnlugh watched from a high place before returning to Cartimandua. He rode toward Isurium, to warn the queen of Venutius and his plots. He rode just in front of Edric, in his blind-spot. But he could see Edric clear as day.

He was ready to move. He thought about all the years he had planned and waited; all the years he had watched Edric as a distant shadow; always waiting for the right time. Edric Bloodeworthe would not stand in his way. Now he was ready to take back that which was his. Now was the time.

CHAPTER FIFTEEN

IMBOLC
Spring

BIANNA AND CAMULO LED the contingency toward Gabrantovices, as Edric had directed. Imbolc was drawing close, and Maawan was heavy with child.

Sadness had spread over the household when Osma and Lucius lost their firstborn. The baby came seven or eight weeks early and had little chance of living. When they arrived back in Gabrantovices, Osma and Lucius took the dead child to the top of the cairn, first wrapping him in white linen, then placing a cross of green reeds tied carefully round his little chest. They walked together to the top of the cairn. There, overlooking the vast Northern Sea, they offered their son to the Roman Gods. Osma wept uncontrollably. Lucius was equally devastated, and unable to relieve her pain.

Bianna felt a heavy sense of disquiet after the death of the child. Imbolc was drawing near, and Maawan was due to give birth any day. Bianna would be glad when Edric returned. She prayed daily to the gods that this baby would be born well. She looked out each day for sign of the return of her brother; only then would she be able to leave the sept to meet Dugall in Ynys Môn.

She had already prepared for the journey.

Donnlugh arrived back at the oppidum of Cartimandua. With speed he burst into her halls.

'My queen,' he greeted, bowing with a flourish. The queen was with two bards who were helping her prepare a speech of blessing with which to greet her people at the feast of Imbolc. She was seated at her throne and was impatient to begin. Her new husband Vellocatus was waiting in her bedroom. She was eager to join him after the fashioning of the oration.

'What is it?' she asked, waving him away with the back of her hand.

'My lady, I have found the traitor, Edric Bloodeworthe. It is he whom defiled your daughter. He is on his way passing Isurium, as we speak.'

The queen rose from her throne. 'Bring him to me!' she growled.

In obedience, Donnlugh marched out of the room, his dark cloak thrashing the air as it swung from side to side. Darkness followed in his wake, bringing nightfall as he left. Heading straight to the warrior shelters, he called six men to arms and set off back toward Edric. They picked up his trail easily, as Edric headed northeast toward a resting place within the settlement farm at Poclin.

Edric greeted a local dairy farmer who agreed to give him shelter for the night. But before he had settled down to sleep, a voice shouted through the roundhouse doorway.

'Queen's Men! Come into the light. All who inhabit this place, come out now, or be drawn!' Torches flooded the room with light, as soldiers entered and circled the room. Edric was first up and standing. With sword drawn, Edric rallied quickly. He looked for a way out, realising he should have done this before settling. There was no escape.

The dairy farmer stood into the light. 'What is this?' he asked, holding his hands up in query. 'What brings you to this outpost?' Two women came into the circle of soldiers holding torches, and stood next to the dairy farmer, huddling close.

Another man, younger than the farmer asked, 'What do you want with us?' He nervously shifted from one foot to the other.

Donnlugh walked into the room. For a moment, his dark stature blocked the light, creating shadows in every corner of the room. The shapes loomed large and formidable, forgathering to cast an enormous silhouette upon the roof. It seemed as if a gigantic spirit from the underworld had entered, bringing fear with him.

"That's him,' called Donnlugh. 'Take him and tie him.'

Donnlugh and his men had surrounded Edric.

'Not without a fight, my lord,' shouted Edric, and his sword was upon two of the soldiers before they had time to realise what he was about. The younger farmer raised his sword to help, but the farmer grabbed his arm.

'No!' he shouted. 'This is not our fight.'

The other soldiers came at Edric. He used all his might to disarm them and get to Donnlugh. His sword sung, cutting wherever the blade touched. Blood spewed over the floor and over the fighting men. Edric couldn't see who he attacked but, in a frenzy, he gashed and sliced whatever stood in the way of the door and his escape. But Donnlugh was ready, dagger in hand. As Edric made for the doorway, Donnlugh made for his arm. Edric dropped his sword as the dagger found its place. He fell, winded. Two of the queen's men grabbed him.

Edric was tossed onto the back of Donn's horse, his hands and feet tied under its belly. The High Druid rode Edric back to Isurium, to the queen.

On arrival at the halls of Cartimandua, Edric was propelled into a small cell like room, where shackles were placed round his wrists and ankles. He was left in squalor, without food or water, until the eve of Imbolc.

His thoughts turned constantly to Maawan. Love and forgiveness swelled in his chest.

'Why was I ever angry with her?' he questioned. Shock hit him hard as he realised that he may never again see Maawan or the child she carried. A tear fell down his cheek. He prayed to the gods for Buite and Beored to burst in on the darkness and free him, but they did not. He was weak. The prison gave his eyes no light. He knew he would stumble in any attempt at escape. He lifted his face upward. Then Donnlugh came.

'Edric Beornraed, High Breehin and Lord of Gabrantovices. Is this you?' he asked. Edric found no sense in lying. It seemed clear to him that the Druid knew exactly who he was.

'I am he.'

'You are the son of Edwin Bloodeworthe.' This seemed like a statement rather than a question, so Edric did not reply. The Druid punched Edric in the jaw. 'Speak,' he threatened, holding his hand to strike again.

'Yes,' answered Edric.

'Then you may know your father and I were brothers. You are Lord of Gabrantovices only because your father stole my patrimony. I am the eldest son of Ogma; Edwin was but a runt in our family.'

Edric dared to ask, 'Then why did you lose your inheritance to him?'

'I was called to greater power,' he spewed. 'I stood by the queen all these years. It suited me to allow Edwin to hold my lands, at that time. But now I require my land be returned to me. I will take the title of Lord of Gabrantovices. '

Edric thought about his father. He knew his father had a reputation for having a ruthless streak, but he could not believe that he would outdo his own brother without just cause. Yet he had no way of knowing the truth of it.

He turned to Donnlugh. 'I would willingly give you my lands, Donnlugh, if they were still mine to give,' he said. 'But my wife is with child, and that child will be heir to my lands and the lands of your queen. You may have chosen power over position, Donnlugh, but power cannot be held in hand for long without becoming a conflagration that burns savagely,' Edric continued, his voice weak. 'The queen, when she receives news of her daughter's condition, will keep hold of the land. It will never be yours.'

The Druid became incensed by those words. He flung his fist into Edric's face, punching him mercilessly until blood rushed from his nose and mouth.

'You dare to come back at me?' he called as he kicked the young warrior in the stomach and chest. Edric cried out in pain as his liver ruptured. 'Do not underestimate my power over the queen. I whisper in her ear, and she acts. Why do you think your father ended up decollated?' he sneered.

Edric spit the blood from his mouth and asked, 'What had my father done to make you so incensed?'

Donnlugh brandished a fist, beating Edric as each word came out of his mouth. 'He took *my* woman! Yes, Edric, your mother was betrothed to *me!*' Donnlugh started to pace round Edric. Rage devoured his senses. 'Cynifrida and her family held the land — I would have gained the ruling hand when Cynifrida and I wed. But Edwin took her. He waited till I was learning my art on Ynys Môn, and he stole her virginity. The result of that union was the sprawling brat that you are!'

Still pacing, he raged, 'I cannot stand the sight of you a moment longer.' Taking his hands to Edric's throat, Donn squeezed hard enough to see Edric's face redden, as the breath in his lungs was expelled. But even amid his rage, he relaxed his grip knowing that he must deliver his captive to the queen. Taking control of his fury, Donnlugh inhaled deeply. Wrapping his cloak round his body, the High Druid ordered calmly, 'Get him before the queen.'

The chains were unlocked and Edric was dragged out of the cell. The wardens threw him into the hall where he fell, prostrate, before the throne.

People were filling the Great Throne Hall of Cartimandua where the royal household and revellers had already begun the celebrations for Imbolc. A huge fire burned brightly in the centre of the room. Candles and torches illuminated the large space. The throne itself was a wonderful piece of ironware in the shape of a trumpet. Long, thin straps of iron, each decorated with runes and wheels, stood side by side, wrapped around a huge barrel shaped wooden structure. Smaller strips of iron formed the front where a seat had been fashioned. Soft cushions lay on the seat; blue and red feather filled balloons. Around the seat, the iron slats grew smoothly, forming a high back which flared out to create a huge fan–like collar.

Donnlugh called for Cartimandua to join them. The queen entered the room and a hush fell among the people. Donnlugh bowed low as she entered. When Cartimandua sat, the collar of the throne seemed to belong to her crown; they became a seamless illusion. The iron had been polished till it shone like silver. The firelight and candles reflected in the metal adding a dazzling array of sparkling radiance to the room.

'As a sacrifice on this feast eve of Imbolc, I have brought before you the undoer of your daughter,' he said. 'This is Edric Bloodeworthe.' He kicked the ensnared warrior to make sure the queen had no doubt about whom he spoke. 'Son of Edwin Bloodeworthe, the traitor who rebelled against your crown, my queen. He was the one you beheaded, as a warning to his people, the Gabrantovices.'

The queen looked at the beaten, blood-soaked man before her. She took her royal sword from the scabbard by the throne, twisting it in her hand. Edric raised his head, though he could not see the queen clearly. Blood running from his lacerations clouded his vision.

'How is my daughter?' she enquired.

'When last I saw her, she was well, queen.' As Edric answered the queen, he drew his knees under his body, and with the little strength he had left, began to press into the floor for support as he lifted himself into a kneeling position.

'Where is she?' she asked.

'She is safe, with my people,' he answered. From somewhere deep within, Edric rallied enough strength to lever his weakened legs. He stood upright in front of the queen, though shaking in pain. Two armed guards moved to flank the enfeebled warrior, should he move toward the queen or try to escape.

Cartimandua signalled to the guards to leave him be, and then turned to Donn Donnlugh.

'Go,' she said. The High Druid swept out of the room. Within the shortest of time, he had mounted his steed and was riding toward Gabrantovices, leading a Centuria of Roman soldiers.

Softly Cartimandua stepped toward Edric. All eyes were on the queen as she spoke.

'What have you to say on this dark night; your last night with breath?'

'One thing I have learned, my queen,' Edric whispered, 'Is when hatred reigns, then death follows. When love is lord, then forgiveness has the upper hand, and life is washed in immortality. Today, though you take my body, you can never take my heart. It has been washed in the eternal love between your daughter and me. This love will outlive you and your High Druid.'

Cartimandua raised her eyebrows as she raised her sword to his throat. Edric looked straight into the queen's eyes. 'It is not through you, but Maawan and I, that Brigantia will live.'

A look of confusion flickered across the queen's face. As Cartimandua met Edric's gaze, her breathing increased; unknown fear rose in her heart. His steady eyes pierced into her very soul. She looked away, unable to engage with him. The guards knocked Edric to the ground.

Cartimandua, taking control of her thoughts once again, turned to face the insolent warrior kneeling before her; this man who had dared to defy her. She raised her sword and rested the weapon on Edric's neck, feeling for the weight of the tool, as she prepared herself for the pleasure to come.

She decreed; 'For your treachery, and your defilement of my daughter; the future queen of Brigantia, this night you will become a sacrifice to Teutates; the god who requires blood.'

As the royal sword fell, lightning struck. In that split second Cartimandua realised what Edric had conveyed; that she had killed the father of her grandchild. But too late.

The *numina,* in response to her actions, threw fire in every direction. The thatch roof of the glorious hall burst into flames, throwing hissing fireballs to every side. The large stone walls were battered as the fireballs circled. Men scattered, trying to avoid the flames.

In her rush to escape the inferno, the queen fell onto Edric's body, covering herself in his blood. His head rolled with the fire, consumed as a blazing inferno. The queen ran, cursing the god of blood and the dragon fire of the *numina* as she fled.

The moon rose high on the night of Imbolc. The candles around the room flickered softly, and the fire in the hearth was bright and warm.

A golden glow lit the bed where Maawan lay.

Her time had come. A pitcher of sea water was by the bed. It had been warming over the fire in readiness. Bianna, following the instructions passed in her vision, offered the water to the gods, sanctified it by adding dried petals of white rose and ground acorns, a spell for protection. All was ready. Bianna stood by Maawan as she cried with the labour pains.

Maawan grabbed hold of Bianna and cried out. 'Where is Edric, Bianna?' she asked, gripping her arm with such ferocity that Bianna thought it would break.

'I do not know, Maawan. But I am sure he will be on his way home. He promised to be here by Imbolc.' Bianna stood by as she cried with the pains of the contractions, and although she wanted to bring comfort to Maawan, she could not, for a burning in her heart told her that something was dreadfully wrong.

'Will this torment ever end?' Maawan shouted, and then, just as suddenly as the pains had started, the baby's head appeared. As the midwife approached to ease the baby out, it seemed that fire had burst out of Maawan's womb. The women took a step back as the baby, without help, broke out of her watery prison, to reveal a golden luminary with fiery red crown. Maawan cried with delight at seeing her daughter in that golden hour.

With the help of the mid woman, Osma took the child and, using the saltwater from the Great Northern Sea, as the gods had decreed, she gently washed the birth vernix away. She wrapped the new-born in soft woven blankets. The tufts of fiery red hair were swaddled into the hood of the tiny cape. Bianna sat with Maawan as she slept lightly, holding her child.

Donnlugh and his hundred men rode with great haste toward Gabrant-ovices. They were almost upon the sept when the guard saw them approach. He sounded the alarm, shouting loud enough to be heard over the sound of galloping horses.

'Enemy approaching! Romans approaching! Get your armour and weapons!' The word went out and warriors lined the inside of the gate. Cerdic hurried to the hall, shouting for Bianna.

'Get her out, Bianna. Get Maawan and the baby out and hide. Romans are coming. You must escape.' Bianna ran to Maawan, imploring her to get up and dress.

'We need to leave,' she begged. 'Osma, take the baby and put her needs in a basket. Take her onto the cairn and wait there for us. Call for

Yetta to help! Quickly now.'

Osma swaddled the child in warm wraps and hurried out to the cairn.

Calling for Lucius and Camulo, Bianna ordered them to go with Osma and protect the babe. Camulo urgently collected packs for the horses, filling them with ample provisions. He led them swiftly and silently to the cairn, while Bianna and Dyn helped Maawan.

As she helped Maawan out of the birth bed, hellish screams and roars could be heard as the noise of slaughter grew. The gates were breeched, and soldiers rode into the sept.

Maawan was weak. Her legs could not hold her. Blood dripped down her legs. She fell to the floor in a faint. Dyn tried to lift her but could not. Bianna had to make a decision, and fast. She looked at Dyn, and Dyn looked back. He knew what she was asking.

'I will stay with her, Bianna. Go with the child. I will hide Maawan.' He spoke with control and authority. 'Go!' he said. Bianna turned to Maawan, 'Sister, I pray for your protection, and for Edric. I will safeguard the child, for she carries the Primogeniture of Brigantia. Fire brings her birth and with fire she will rule.'

As she passed the baby to Bianna, Maawan whispered, 'Her name will be Brighid; born as the winter becomes summer, born with fire to illuminate and with wisdom to bring blessing. This war will not be in vain. The spirit of Brigantia lives in my daughter.'

Bianna kissed her sister, as Maawan pressed into her hand the signet ring of Brigantia. With a bow, Bianna fled the room and fled the sept.

Dyn pulled Maawan into a corner of the room, where Bianna's clothes chest stood. He opened it and helped Maawan climb inside, then covered her with Edric's red ceremonial cloak. Dyn bolted the high oak doorway before hiding behind the bed.

The soldiers ransacked and killed as they rode through the village. Heading toward the main hall, Donnlugh indicated to his men to advance. Donnlugh dismounted as they approached the doorway. Ten or so of the soldiers followed as he searched the now empty hall. They swept through the rooms to find them empty. The soldiers began to barrage the fastened oak door, bombarding it until the hinges began to falter. They continued ramming while others fetched an iron spear to use as leverage under the weakened lock, till the door burst open.

Scanning the room, Donnlugh went to the chest. The red cloak hid Maawan well, but not well enough. Donnlugh lifted the cloak, leaving nothing to chance. When he saw Maawan; and the pool of blood she was lying in, paired with the defiant look on her face, he asked, 'Where is the child?'

'Where is Edric, Donn Donnlugh?' responded Maawan.

'I left him with your mother, princess. He will be without his head by now.' Donnlugh smirked as he spoke. 'And you, my lady, are going to meet him, unless you tell me where the child is.'

'The child died. He is already with the gods. And I would be happy to follow — to know that I would be united with my soul spirit.' Maawan lied. 'Do your worst Donnlugh! Now, take me to my mother, the queen,' she ordered.

'Keep your voice steady,' she told herself. 'You have the authority here.'

Dyn, from his hiding place, silently stretched his arm round toward the bedside where a dagger lay. Worming round the bed, he reproached himself. 'I am useless.' he thought. Why did I not have *my* dagger with me?'

Donnlugh looked straight into Maawan's eyes. Hatred oozed from him. 'You can't avoid me, little princess.' He offered his hand, as she moved to step out of the closet.

Maawan looked toward Donnlugh, meeting him eye to eye. 'Is that a flicker of doubt in his expression?' she thought. Donnlugh took her hand as if to help her. She reached to take it.

'Did you really think that I would take you to your mother?' he laughed as he grabbed her wrist. 'I will be rid of you; and her!'

Dyn silently took the dagger.

Maawan understood instantly, the feelings she had experienced while still a child, growing up under Donnlugh's dark and sinister gaze. She had seen his hatred for her; he breathed it whenever he was near. He breathed the same hatred for Cartimandua, even as he served her.

The veil in front of Maawan's eyes had been torn away, leaving only a clear view of the dark lord; a manifestation of power-grabbing avarice.

Reaching into his cloak for his dagger, with lightning speed, Donnlugh thrust his blade into Maawan's heart. Dyn jumped from his hiding place, and with frenzied force, he stabbed Donnlugh in the back and kidneys. Again and again, Dyn stabbed until Donnlugh fell.

The Roman soldiers did not spare a moment. Rushing to capture Dyn, they cut him down swiftly. The Druid dropped at the side of his mistress. The destructive wildfire from the Roman torches spread high over Gabrantovices.

The flames rose high from the lord's hall and over the land.

CHAPTER SIXTEEN

YNYS MÔN
The Holy Isle

SUETONIUS PAULINUS SENT a legion: where there had been ten Romans, there were now thousands. Marching toward Ynys Môn from Deva, they placed the Druids firmly in their sights.

'Destroy the Druid colony and Brigantia will fall. Their religion holds them. Destroy that power source, and you will have the people,' Paulinus ordered. 'It is a haven for heretics, savages, and barbarians. We will bring their end and the end to the Druid rule.'

The army left Deva, marching toward the Sychnant Pass. Paulinus ordered Albion slaves, bound by irons, to construct flat bottomed boats to be hewn from single trunks of oak. The mainland and Combrogi was separated from the isle of Ynys Môn by a narrow strip of water, and although the crossing would be a short and fairly easy one, it depended on the tides. These boats would be sufficiently robust to counter the strong cross-currents. The taskmasters whipped and tortured the captive Britons until a fleet of boats was ready to take the armies across the waters.

Paulinus sent his men to find guides from the local areas, to take the legions across the water. They garrisoned near the Laven Sands, preparing to cross in their hordes.

Bianna and the others gathered momentarily on the cairn. Bianna picked a winter rose from the ground and placed it inside the child's blanket before they all mounted their horses, spurring forward with haste. Osma held the child, sitting behind Lucius and hanging onto him as he quickened his pace. They journeyed toward the outskirts of Isurium, avoiding septs and villages. They travelled southwest, without daring to look back.

The horses began to tire as they approached a small village on the edge of the Brigantium border. Camulo signalled for the group to lay low behind a copse of tall trees by a river, until he had surveyed the area. Osma dismounted the horse and sat with the babe in her arms. Lucius carefully covered them in a blanket, as Osma cradled the whimpering infant. The milk from her breasts found its way to its hungry mouth. The soft nuzzle of the searching mouth comforted Osma in her loss.

Camulo arrived back, with a plan for rest that night. Legeolium was a trading sept, and although he had seen Romans wandering through the houses, they seemed not to be with arms or armour. 'Lucius,' Camulo turned to the roman, 'can you lead us in and help us find rest?' he asked.

'I will,' he answered, helping Osma and her bundle to rise from the ground.

They followed Lucius into the sept. The gated entrance was just about to be closed for the night, but no one ventured to ask who they were or where they had come from. The open shelters near the horse compounds cost a few coins, which Camulo handed over freely, so they were able to rest safely. Leaving Lucius with Osma and the child, the others set out to buy food and water and to evaluate the situation they found themselves in.

The news of the sacking of Gabrantovices had not yet travelled to Legeolium, so for a while, at least, they allowed themselves to relax. As they ate their meagre meal of bread and cheese, Lucius asked where they were bound for, and if Bianna had a plan.

'I will travel down to Ynys Môn to meet with Dugall there,' she said. 'I will take the child to the Druid holy isle, and perhaps beyond, to Iberio,' she explained. She knew that she would be traveling the way of danger, and past visions played in her mind. 'I must find Dugall,' she thought. 'Together we will find a way through this madness. The gods have led us thus far. I will trust our gods for protection, till they compete their purposes.' Looking at Lucius, her expression begged, 'Osma, Lucius; will you travel with me a little further? Then you are all free to go where the wind takes you.'

Camulo was the first to speak. 'It seems madness to me, Bianna, but I know you have abilities beyond my understanding. May I have your permission to return home, to Ellestob? I miss Raegan and would go to her. I will come at your calling whenever you bid, should you ever need me,' he promised. Bianna nodded her consent.

Yetta spoke next. 'I will ride a little way with you tomorrow, Bianna, until I reach Beored and the others. They will be heading home, and I would like to intercept their journey; to warn them before they see our sept and the destruction wrought upon our homes.' Bianna nodded in agreement at this request too.

'Osma, what will you do when we part ways?' asked Bianna. Osma looked at the child. Tears filled her eyes. The pain she felt at that moment overwhelmed her. Lucius spoke for her.

'My lady, I would like to take Osma to my settlement; the place I have called home for so many years. I promise to care for her, and, if she will have me, I will marry her. We will come with you for the next few days, and then we will circle round to Parisii.' He bowed before the priestess, holding his right hand against his heart.

When the morning came, Camulo waved farewell as he left Legeolium. The others moved in a different direction, taking the west path toward Deva.

Following the hidden paths, resting only for a short time at Outlane, they continued toward Mamucium. It was on this stretch of the journey that Yetta left. She received news from the beer house at Outlane that Brigante warriors had passed by only that day, on their way home: one of them was called Beored.

From there on, they travelled under the cover of night; by-passing Mamucium, they ventured west toward the great Mamu-cium River, then south. As they saw Deva in the distance, along with the swarms of soldiers moving as one great company. They knew that they had to travel swiftly, and before the swarms burst out of the hive.

Passing the baby to Bianna, Lucius and Osma bade farewell. Bianna knew the way she would take to Ynys Môn. The path had been routed well in advance. Dugall was calling; she could hear him on the wind. She rode on until she reached the sands, hoping that she would be with him before the imminent danger was unleashed.

Hiding from the troops already assembling on the seafront, she looked for a guide. She knew one would be working close by, so she headed toward a few small boats tied to a breaker. She called out to a swarthy man who was busy loading a few casks into the bottom of his shallow draft boat. 'Ynys Môn?' she asked.

'Ynys Môn,' he nodded. Without saying more, she stepped into the boat. 'We will catch the tides if we leave straight away,' he said and began to push the boat out to sea. 'Lie low in the bottom,' he instructed. The child was cold and getting hungry, but Bianna knew that she would soon be at the refuge, the planned meeting place of safety. She had but a little way to go when the boat landed on the isle. Giving the boatman a coin, she thanked him and began to run up the hill.

The enemy hordes gathered, ready to cross the torrid waters from the mainland to the holy Isle. The Druids and people of the island gathered on the hilltop overlooking the shore.

Women in black clothing, waving brands of fire, ran with frenzied wrath, weaving in and out between the Druid lines. They chanted in the old tongue, words of curse and warnings of doom. Druids lifted their arms and began incantations till dreadful curses and obscenities rode on the wind so fiercely that the deafening sound caused a wave of terror among the landing infantries. Their limbs froze from the dread of seeing this mighty malediction.

The leaders of the landing army rode among the petrified Roman soldiers; many falling as they were struck by shooting spears, arrows, and stones. They tried to rally the fearful men.

'They are but caterwauling women! No need to be fearful of the black-cloaked Druids. They are mere men!' they called.

'Forward, army. Forward!' came the command. The Roman soldiers gathered their strength and began to move again towards the gathered Druid clans.

With ferocious strength and force, they advanced toward the Druid line. With fire and sword, they fought the Druids. Slashing and killing the priesthood who battled for their lives, the Romans furthered their ground. Banshees danced and wailed, watching as every last one of them was massacred. The fires blazed on all who stood in the way of the butchers from Rome.

Bianna stumbled in the hill fog as she made her way toward the agreed meeting place.

Looking back, she could see the flames of the conflict growing higher. She moved as quickly as she was able, holding the babe in her basket tightly in her arms. Rain poured and the wind blew; the stormy turmoil soaking the cloak she wore. Before long, her spirits, like her cloak, became overwhelmed. It was then that the Druid malaise dropped like a magic mist. Tiredness and trance overtook

Bianna, as she danced in a weary stupor; all the time trying to keep her body upright and her feet moving.

With one trip, the basket and child had gone.

Bianna fell to the ground, weeping and crying. The darkness had taken over. Great sadness and defeat swept over Bianna, as she tried desperately to climb out of the hole she had fallen into. It seemed as if time had been eaten away. The world had gone into slow motion. Nothing…nothing…except darkness…

Through the darkness of the mist, Bianna strained her eyes. Her exhaustion was complete, and the heaviness of loss and defeat weighed her down. The blackness was so dense it appeared like a high impenetrable wall that Bianna hadn't the strength to climb.

She felt her way round the thickness, like a blind person feeling for escape. Shadows lurked here and there, as if they were looking for other lost souls. Then her view shifted as in a dream.

The wall before her became flexible; yielding, like drapes of fabric mist swirling; spinning her round. She could feel the touch of the folds. She was holding the blackness in her hands.

'The cloak of Donn,' she thought, looking at her hands in horror. An intense heat from the mantle made her hands feel as if they were on fire. As if she would be defiled by it, she dropped it, and observing from her trancelike distance, she saw the smouldering robe as it drifted downward from her grasp, into the mouth of a pit. It floated away into the underworld, on its returned to Arwan, the god of death. The soul of Donnlugh entering the murky abyss of night was no more.

A flash of light made Bianna look up. Dugall Dubthach, shining like a star in the heavens, flew above the chasm. In his hand a golden staff with *Breo saighead ;* the fiery arrowhead flashed into the shadows as he damned the High Druid to the realm of *Damnadh.* A beam of lightning power shot into the sky illuminating the firmament, and the shadow was gone.

Behind the night fog, dawn was edging forward.

A single candle flame appeared as a beam of light. 'Bianna,' a voice called… 'Bianna, I am here.'

Bianna gasped at the sound. 'Dugall?' she called back. 'Is that you, Dugall?' From out of the clouded gloom and darkness, a solitary figure emerged.

'Yes, Bianna, it is me.'

Dugall moved out of the mist toward the dazed woman on her knees. He stretched out his arm and wrapped it round his wife, lifting her easily from the hole she had stumbled into.

'Oh, Dugall! I fear Edric may be dead, and Maawan; gone. Our world is burned! I lost the child — I lost Brighid!' sobbed Bianna, overcome with anguish.

'Come. I have the child safely. Quickly now! The boat is ready to take us to *Eriu*, to safety. The fires of our world burn and the enemy will soon be upon us. We must leave now!' he said with urgency. As Dugall helped Bianna, he continued to encourage her. 'Edric is indeed gone, my love. Through a dream, I saw his murder. While Edric fought for his life, I was fighting Donn in the underworld,' he explained. 'He has been banished to the place of shadows.' As he spoke, Dugall directed Bianna onwards.

'So the old must die? Everything we have? Everything we are?' cried Bianna, as she thought about her brother.

'Our world and ancient ways are being torn from us. There is a new world on the horizon. These two worlds cannot sit side by side. They collide, bringing chaos. We fight, but it only compounds the turmoil. The old has to die to allow the new to find its place, so the eternal wheel of life will turn.' He pulled Bianna close and from beneath his cloak, safely snuggled, was the child. He handed her to Bianna.

Together they hurried to the waiting boat. Dugall whispered Bianna's ear. 'These invaders may burn our lands and destroy our world, Bianna, but because of this anguish the spirit of Brigantia will only continue to burn more brightly. They may try to quench the fire of passion in the hearts of the Brigante, but it will never be extinguished. These fires burned in the hearts of Edric and Maawan, and they burn in our hearts also. From the ashes, we will be reborn.'

Holding both Bianna and her ward closely, Dugall looked back over the flames burning the sacred place. 'Do your worst, Roman invaders. The fiery spirit of Brigantia will never die.'

Holding the baby together, Bianna lifted her eyes to look at Dugall.

'This is the purpose of our gods!' she said, with understanding. Then, turning to the heavens, she lifted the baby, 'Behold: I give you the eternal flame of Brigantia. I give you Brighid!'

THE LEGEND

Brighid, the Goddess of the Eternal Fire and Warfare [Briga], was the Goddess of Brigante warriors. Her name means 'Exalted One.'

Brighid was said to be the daughter of Dubthach, a Druid who brought her from The Druid Holy Isle to Ireland.

Brighid is also known as Breo-Saighit: The Fiery Arrow. When she was born, it is told, a tower of flame erupted, reaching from the top of her head to the heavens, and giving the house of her birth the appearance of being on fire.

Brigit's birthday is Imbolc, celebrated on or close to February 1st, marking the end of the darkness and the coming of the light and spring. She is the Goddess of cows and their milk, fertility, healing, landscape, oak groves, and holy wells. Her flame, it is said, is eternal — celebrating the continuity of the old traditions as they changed and reshaped into the Christian traditions. Possibly through syncretism, Brighid became the Christian: St Brigid of Ireland.

Today, Brighid is seen as the warrior, Brigantia; the personification of Britain holding the symbols of justice and authority over the realm.

TIMELINE

36AD

• Edric Beornraed, Lord Bloodeworthe of Gabrantovice is born.
•Son of Edwin and Cynifrida.

38AD

•Bianna Bloodeworthe, priestess, Druid warrior is born.
•Daughter of Lord Edwin and Cynifrida, sister of Edric.
•Queen of Brigantia meets Eachann Beli Mawr, chief warrior of the tribal head Venutius of Carvetti.
•They have twin daughters that year.

40AD

•A third child, princess Maawan is born to Queen Cartimandua and Eachann.

43AD

•Cartimandua marries Venutius, and their respective tribes, headed by Queen Cartimandua and Venutius as her consort king are united.
•Her three daughters are removed for safety by Camulo and brought up for three years by his wife Raegan before being returned to their mother.

44AD

•Cartimandua surrenders to the Roman invaders but retains her crown and lands. This arrangement with the Romans brings her much wealth, and the lives of her people area spared.
•In return for favours granted by the Romans, she on their behalf, protects the northern borders of Brigantia from marauding Picts and Gaels.

•This allows the Romans to concentrate on their occupation of the southern areas of Britannia.
•The pact that the queen made with the Romans angered some, causing factions of Brigante to rise against her.

50AD
•Cartimandua beheads Edwin Bloodeworthe for his insurrection, sending his decapitated body home to Gabrantovices as a warning.

51AD
•Caracatus battles against the Roman invasion of Wales.
•He escapes Roman capture and goes to Cartimandua for protection.
•She betrayed him, presenting him in shackles, as a gift to the Romans.
•They reward her with great wealth.

55AD
•Cynifrida dies. Edric kills Taexalin and becomes Lord of Gabrantovices.

56AD
•Venutius enlarges his war against the Roman Protectorate, building alliances outside Brigantia.

57AD
•Cartimandua has an affair with her husband's chariot servant, Vellocatus.
•She divorces Venutius and marries Vellocatus. Civil war breaks out among the Brigante people, dividing Cartimandua and her Roman allies against Venutius. Cartimandua takes the family of Venutius as hostages.

58AD
•Bianna marries Dugall Dubthach.

59AD
•Edric marries Maawan Biann.

60AD
•Edric supports Venutius at the battle of Deva.

61AD

•Ynys Môn is ransacked by the Romans. Boudicca rebels against the Romans because of the destruction of Ynys Môn.
•The old religion is decimated.

CELTIC SEASONS

Samhain : Beginning of winter and the New Year — *1st November.*
          Representing the final harvest before winter sets in.
          A time to honour ancestors and embrace the dark half of the
          year.

Yule   : Midwinter — *20th / 24th December.*
          The shortest day of the year.

Imbolc : Beginning of Spring — *1st February.*
          The festival of light, purification, fertility, and new beginnings.

Ostara : Spring Equinox — *20th - 23rd March*
          Time to prepare for the new yearly cycle, and new life.

Beltane : Beginning of summer — *1st May.* Festival celebrating fertility.
          A season of passion, fire, and abundance.

Litha   : Summer Solstice — *20th - 23rd June.*
          The longest day. Celebration of light over darkness

Lughnas : Beginning of autumn / Harvest *1st August.*
          A Festival of fire, celebrating harvest.

Glossary

Aithria	: Rite, tradition.
Alae	: Roman cavalry
A' Lorg	: Gaelic meaning searching
Anam Cara	: Soul
Ambaxtoi	: War leader's immediate companions
Bael	: Pyre or bonfire
Barp	: A mound or cairn of stones
Beannachd leibd	: Gaelic meaning goodbye
Belatucadrus	: God of death also called "fair shining one" or "fair slayer"
Beornraed	: Chief Warrior. Shield of the people.
Boann	: Celtic goddess, princess
Boar-ring	: Arena for fighting boar or other wild animals
Braccae	: A type of drawstring trouser
Braint	: Aristocratic, highly born, noble, strong.
Breehin	: Prince
Breo-Saighead	: Fiery power, or fiery arrowhead.
Brigga	: Goddess of fire, power, and strength
Burraidh	: Idiot, asshead
Caim	: A prayer for safety and blessing
Cailleach	: Goddess of disease, plagues, and destruction among other things.
Carnyx	: A type of bronze trumpet
Combrogi	: Land of compatriots – Cymru
Cornu	: An ancient Roman trumpet
Couchen	: Drink made from mead and fermented honey
Damnadh	: Damnation
Drueidan	: Sacred Druid languag
Dyn Hysbys	: Wizard, knower of spells
Dwam	: Trance, daydream, stupor

Ecnaire	: Druid funeral rite
Egregore	: Collective mind, a meme
Eques	: Scouts and messengers of Roman army
Eriu	: Celtic name for Ireland
Fey	: Druid wand, magical staff
Fibula	: Brooch
Filid	: Druid bards and poets who recorded events in song and poetry
Folgiere	: Follower
Galea	: Roman helmets
Geidd	: Story, tale, song, or poem
Gearr	: Sacred hare /rabbit
Golden Plover	: Golden Plover
Grainne	: Sunshine. A term of endearment
Heofan	: Sky, heavens
Hrycg	: Ancient name meaning 'the top or crest'
Legatus Legionis	: Commanding officer of Roman Legion
Lige	: To lie
Numerus	: Unit of Barbarian allies
Numina	: A spirit or divine power over a thing or place
Obsequies	: Funeral rites
Ogham	: Celtic tree alphabet
Oppidum	: Fortified town, especially one under Roman rule
Rick	: Stack of hay or wood
Saorsa	: Freedom, liberty
Sgilean Dorca	: Dark Shadow
Scate	: Base liar, ne'er-do-well, fantasist
Sept	: Settlement of roundhouses. A village or town
Sith	: Experience, journey
Sluagh-ghairm	: Army war cry
Steinvegges	: Stone walled settlement
Taranis	: Celtic god of thunder and the wheel
Triarius	: Ancient Roman Soldiers
Tunskipe	: Township
Uabhais	: Fear, terror

ACKNOWLEDGEMENTS

I have just celebrated my seventieth birthday, and not once in all those years, did I ever imagine that I would hold my own book in my hand. Over those years, I talked a lot about the possibility; about the stories in my head, but I never got round to writing them. But here I am, finally with a completed story. I realise that I could not have done this without the help, generosity, and support from so many of my friends and family.

Grateful thanks for the support and professional expertise that the DreamEngine team supplied; especially David Baboulene, Edward Marsh, and Emma Julian. Their encouragement and support allowed me the privilege to indulge in the prospect of becoming a published author. You are brilliant.

Special thanks to my team of readers, editors, and story improvers – Ann Mapplebeck, Laura Hudson Mackay, Scott Mackay, Rosemary Bowyer, Paul Bowyer, Vicki Frost, Steve Frost, and Maria Holland.

Thanks to the very talented, Louise Todd for the wonderful illustrations, and to Laura Hudson Mackay for her work on my website. I will always be grateful for your love and support. I send a big hug.

And finally, a big thank you and a big smackeroo to my ever loving, ever patient husband, Kevin. He doesn't know what he would do without me.

I don't know what I would do without him.

ABOUT THE AUTHOR

Tina is a Yorkshire woman who personifies the spirit of Queen Cartimadua. She has firm principles based on the philosophy that a person has to put energy into life if they are going to get anything out of life.

Her positivity is infectious and she is both inspiring and active in helping people to lead a happy life. She is particularly interested in helping older people to continue to feel happy and fulfilled.

Tina uses the power of storytelling, the richness of history, and the place of women central to authentic stories to inspire others to be true to themselves in the world today. In a world where history is sacrificed on the altar of political correctness, Tina questions the need to change those stories, but rather learn from them.

Twitter: Tina_Zee_111
Facebook: Tina Zee
Website: Tina Zee

Have you got a book in you? Want to get published?

DreamEngine provides extraordinary support for aspiring authors who want education, expert marketing, and an author mythology that actually sells books. Talk to us today!

publishing@dreamengine.co.uk

dreamengine.co.uk

ALSO BY DREAMENGINE

Ocean Boulevard
by David Baboulene

An epic and exhilarating journey all the way...from a boy to a man. If PG Wodehouse had gone to sea...

Jumping Ships
by David Baboulene

What more do you need to know than what other people think? If PG Wodehouse had joined the Merchant Navy...

Fires of Brigantia
by Tina Zee

The Roman army. One Yorkshire woman. They never stood a chance.

Surface
by Violet neill

Book 1 of the Hollow Trilogy. Lucas Spencer loves his wife Adele. She is beautiful, intellegent... And dead.

Life's a Peach
by Steve Askham

Extraordinary fruity business you didn't know that you NEED to know... The secret life of an international fruit trader.

The Magical World of Lilly Lemoncello
by Carolyn Goodyear

Fate decides Lilly's start in life. So she chooses to let Fate decide the rest of it too. A heartwarming and remarkable work of human goodness.

The Shock Tube
by Paul Curtis
Anybody reading this book will learn something uncomfortable.
About themselves...

Nonfiction:

The Story Series
by David Baboulene
Learn how stories work.

Printed in Great Britain
by Amazon

80722706R00109